THE MONA LISAS

Carl R Stokes

FOR. PHIL.
MAPPY BIRTHDAY.

HOPE YOU ENJY.

PROLOGUE

He had entered by the visitor's entrance, and the musty smell of this place assaulted his nostrils. Standing in the centre of the place always made him feel like being in the stomach of a whale, this place being just as much a living thing.

He was here after receiving a phone call which had interrupted his morning's work of paper plane production. Business was quiet at the moment. From his second floor office above the charity shop he could see the place he now stood in.

The gist of the call was to meet Lily here and all would become clear. The voice on the phone was that of a younger woman.

He knew of Lily by reputation only, and that was as big as the whole city.

Lily would now be in her mid seventies but in her heyday was the most famous prostitute in the city. The City having a barracks on its doorstep for over one hundred years, the oldest profession had always flourished.

What she would want with him, a fledgling PI in a Staffordshire cathedral city, he hadn't a clue. But as he had got through half a ream of paper and it was still only eleven am, the five hundred yard walk from his office would save his sanity and his paper.

It was now spring and he had left the police force the previous summer in a fit of pique. Too much paper work, not enough support and no confidence that if he put someone behind bars that they would not be out on good behaviour with only half their time served. The system was mad.

The message was to meet by one of the private chapels that clung to the side the cathedral. As he approached he saw a well dressed woman in her mid twenties leaning over to speak to a woman sitting on an electric four wheel scooter, the sort that run you over in shopping centres. They both looked up on seeing him approach.

Charlie walked over to them.

The younger one spoke first with an accent he wasn't expecting, not upper class but well bred.

"Charlie Edwards?"

"Yes"

"I'm Zoe and this is my grandmother Lily. She is going to talk to you but I would ask you not to interrupt, as she is not in the best of health and must not get excited. Save your question for later."

Charlie nodded, wondering what he was letting himself in for.

The old lady pointed at him.

"You know who I am then?"

"Yes"

"Reputation is a great thing" she laughed, which ended up as a wheezy cough. Zoe motioned towards her but Lily waved her off.

"I'm ok, I'm ok, let's begin at the beginning"

Charlie could see that she was warming to the task.

"Charlie I have had an interesting life and through it all there has only been one constant, my family. Zoe, her mother and father and James Barker."

Charlie raised an eyebrow at the name because the Barker family were regarded as the local landed gentry.

"He was Lord Lieutenant of Staffordshire when I met him. Through a client, as I think they call them today, I got an invitation to the Hunt Ball, which in the nineteen fifties was the place to be seen. During the night we danced together and just hit it off. Our relationship went from strength to strength. My only fear was that he would find out who I was or that he would ask me to marry him. You see I knew that it would never work, back then the class system was too strong, it would have damaged him and his family.

But as it was events intervened. I fell pregnant with Sheila. He begged me to let him marry me, I told him he couldn't, he asked why. I told him why and he broke down and cried in front of me."

Lily dabbed the corner of her eye with a tissue, Zoe moved towards her, but was waved off.

"He was such a gentleman all his life. Set me up in a flat and paid for everything while I went through the nine months. Sheila was born and he was there. He brought us home from the hospital and popped in to see us as much as he could.

After the first month I made my mind up to tell him not to call again, he had a life to lead and I didn't want him to call on us if he didn't want to."

The tissue came into view again, this time to blow her nose, the noise of which resounded round the cathedral. Charlie looked about but no one seemed to notice. He turned back to Lily.

"In the end we agreed that he would help support her and that I wouldn't take a penny from him. He set up a trust fund for her to go to a private school but when it came to it she hated it. Sheila was bright but not university material, at least not in those days. She had what you would call a middle class childhood and as a teenager in the late sixties was a bit of a hippy. She fell in the end for Teddy. He was an accountant, they married and a year later Sheila fell pregnant with Zoe."

Charlie saw the young woman's neck go red.

"James transferred the trust to Zoe for her education. Only James knew what was in the fund at that time."

Time for a new tissue. Charlie was wondering where this was going and why he was being subjected to it.

"In 2000, Sheila and Teddy were killed in a car accident. By then my condition had been diagnosed and I was living with them up on the hill. Zoe came back from London to look after me."

Charlie had promised not to speak but he was losing his patience.

"Which brings us to why you are here,"

'Finally' thought Charlie.

"James passed away six months ago. He never married. He told me years ago why. He could never marry and not have Sheila as part of his life and he didn't think it would be fair to his bride to have a ready-made daughter. Such a sweet man."

Yes the tissue was out again.

"He had other women in his life but always pulled away before they got too close. Anyway we were called to the reading of the will. Only six people. He gave money to charity. His household retainers were well looked after and there was a niece who didn't look too impressed with what she got. Then there were us two. What we got was a mystery, Charlie, a mystery.

It's about a painting which came into his family in the nineteen twenties.

He had shown me the picture years ago and he called it "The Barker Folly".

In his later life he decided to look into the history of the painting. You see it is a copy of a famous painting, but the more James looked into it the more he thought there was a real chance that it was the genuine article. He established that apart from his, there are three more copies somewhere. He ran out of time before he could find them. Now it's our job to finish what he started. We have to find those other three paintings. To help us we have his papers and a large sum of money. So this is the deal, there is a pot of money we will inherit minus what ever it costs to find the other three owners. We do not get a penny until the other owners are found.

So Charlie, the question is, are you interested in helping us?"

"Well I'm intrigued, but I have some questions."

"Ok."

"Why me?"

"I beg your pardon"

"Why pick on me to contact?"

"Well Charlie, many years ago Sheila was trying to make friends after deciding she didn't want to stay at the private school. She had been there long enough to get a plummy accent and got picked on for it. Just one girl befriended her. Her name was April."

"My Mom?"

"Yes that's right. My chest is tightening up with the musty smell in here, I must go. We will call you tomorrow."

Lily turned the key on her electric scooter, gripped the handlebars and stamped on the accelerator.

Charlie said. "But what is the picture?"

But Lily was disappearing up the ramp and through the exit.

Zoe was trying to keep up with her grandmother while balancing on high heels on the uneven floor. She looked over her shoulder and mouthed something to him that looked like morning Lisa.

Charlie walked to the entrance and squinted in the sunlight, muttering to himself as he went.

'Morning Lisa, well it was just still morning but his name wasn't Lisa, what the hell was she saying?'

Charlie started mouthing Morning Lisa to himself as he passed through the old city gateway into Dam Street.

Suddenly he stopped as he got to Minster Pool and shouted "Mona Lisa".

PART ONE

CHAPTER ONE
MAURETANIA
1910

The face in the mirror smiled back at him. He was going to enjoy this evening. Eduardo knew that his looks had changed over the last ten years. Now at the age of fifty he was fostering the professorial look rather than the Don Juan image he had created since his mid twenties.

Marques Eduardo de Valfierno left his cabin and headed for the dining room.

The Mauretania, the sister ship of the Lusitania, was the grandest ship he had ever seen. He travelled from Argentina on a packet steamer and now travelled from New York to Europe in the lap of luxury. While the opulence and splendour of the journey was very acceptable, the reason for travelling on this ship was purely business. Tonight he would dine with Captain John Pritchard at his table. In his area of the art world, contacts were his lifeblood, and tonight he would be Dracula. He knew who would be at the table, how much they were worth, and their likes and dislikes. He was ready to engage, to put all the years of self-training into practice. He lived for nights like this.

Eduardo had spent his time in Buenos Aires selling obscure paintings by famous artists to wealthy collectors. The sort of private collectors that knew the painting should be in a museum but would pay top Dollar to have them in their homes. The only problem being was that the real paintings were in their rightful museums. Eduardo had only ever sold copies.

The time was right to leave South America after their last sale went wrong.

He sold a painting, which had been stolen from a gallery in Spain. The gallery had very poor security and there was a national outcry. Of course the painting Eduardo sold was a copy. This was fine until the gallery recovered the painting and the story appeared in the press. His purchaser took some convincing that he had sold him the original and that the gallery had commissioned a copy to cover their blushes. The purchaser's own vanity about his knowledge of art playing a big part in the deception.

The writing was on the wall. He had to think of his associate Yves Chaudron.

They had met by chance in a café and hit it off straight away. They both had a passion for art but were complete opposites in personality, Eduardo the extrovert and Yves the introvert. It had begun with a wager that Yves couldn't reproduce a passable copy of one of the Masters? When he did, Eduardo sold it to a tourist and their enterprise had begun.

They decided to make more copies and sell them to tourists. This was profitable for both of them and developed one day when Eduardo was approached by a man of means and asked if he could paint something a little less obvious, something he could show to dinner guests and impress them. The commission was undertaken and they moved into a whole other world. Yves took every painting as a challenge and over the years mastered the techniques of the Masters.

Now it was time to move on and for Eduardo, thoughts of retiring entered his mind. He had had enough of the greedy self obsessed people he had to deal with. One final big charade. One final challenge for Yves.

Eduardo had shipped Yves off to Europe two weeks ago, with instructions to rent a studio in Montmartre. Then create a portfolio of tourist studies of Paris as a cover. Eduardo would wait for the right ship with the right passengers before leaving New York .

As he entered the dining room, he lowered his glasses down the bridge of his nose and started to peer over them. His old school teacher used to do this when dissatisfied with the students. Eduardo had mastered it in the mirror together with a slight stooping of the shoulders. The effect was to make him look ten years older and more scholarly.

The introductions were made. The Wall St banker and his wife, George and Edith Adams. He thin faced, greying at the temples and looking distinctly like he would like to be elsewhere; she very pretty, blonde with an inquisitive gleam in her eyes and at least ten years his junior. They were on their way to see Europe for the first time.

The English Earl, Spencer Harcourt –Smythe. In his early forties with a mane of hair that went down to his shoulders, with steely blue eyes and the look of a man that had lived life to the full and was still pushing the limits, never having to obey the rule of the ordinary man. He was on his way home after visiting relatives in America.

The Austrian wine grower and his wife, Hans and Lotti Teidermar. He was in his late fifties, bald with a goatee beard. His eyebrow had grown into wings, which gave him the look of the devil, this Eduardo was sure he cultivated. She was a good four inches taller and six inches wider than he and possessing the manliest laugh of the people gathered this evening. They were returning home after visiting their American agents.

And finally the Texan oil baron and his wife, Chuck and Avril Parker. He, short and loud, was trying to be the centre of attention. His clothes were expensive but he did not know how to wear them. She was attractive, quiet and elegant. They were going to mix business with pleasure in London.

Eduardo was introduced as an art expert and dealer.

Eduardo had mastered the art of taking part in one conversation and listening to the others round the table. Many think they can do this, but few are able. The usual opening topics about the weather, the ship and the service on board went round the table. Then the conversation went on to questions about what people did when not crossing the Atlantic on the Mauretania. The question went round the table in a clockwise direction, Eduardo taking in the replies, for the best part the information married up with what he knew. When it was his turn, he was asked by the banker's wife if he had a gallery in London. His heart skipped a beat as he baited the trap.

"No Madam. The paintings I deal in are not for the general public to look at through a plate glass window, they are far too valuable."

Being a little put out by the tone of the reply, her husband stepped in with a question of his own

"Then how do you sell these valuable paintings?"

"Sir, there are a lot of paintings in private collections that you would normally think were in museums. When the owner wants to sell them, maybe because the stock market has let him down, or he gambles a little too vigorously, he wants to sell them discreetly. I offer that service and as well as having clients who collect a certain painter's work. So if a painting comes on the market they will ask me to authenticate it for them."

The banker's wife was now intrigued

"And that is what you were doing in New York?"

Eduardo could have kissed her.

"Alas my journey was to no avail as once I had offered my credentials, the owner refused to let me see the painting"

"So you scared him off?"

"It happens sometimes"

"It must be frustrating to have a wasted journey"

"Madam the journey on this fine ship with such fine company as I have tonight is never wasted"

With that Eduardo raised his glass and toasted the table. A perfect result, now he had to be patient, but he knew they would come, like bees to a honeypot.

After the port Eduardo excused himself and took a tour of the deck. The evening was perfect. He had achieved all he intended. All he could do now was to wait. He pondered on which one of them would make contact first. It wouldn't be the Texan; his wife would be the instigator and would work on her husband over the next day or so. The vineyard owner may not have the money to play his game but he had been wrong before. The banker will be cautious; they only like to spend other people's money unless it's a sure thing. Now the Earl is difficult. Nobility are always difficult to read. Some are poor as paupers but manage to retain a façade of prosperity. But in this case he was sure the money was there.

He walked down the companionway towards his cabin. A steward was knocking on the door as he approached. He had a note on a silver tray.

Eduardo thanked the steward, entering his cabin before unfolding the note.

"Well, well, well, that's a turn up for the books!"

He laughed to himself and reread the note.

"I would be pleased if you could join me in the Verandah Café, eleven am tomorrow for a mutually interesting meeting"

The note was signed A. P.

CHAPTER TWO

PARIS

Eduardo looked at the other faces in the compartment. They all wished they were elsewhere. The train from Calais to Paris had left the station an hour ago, moved five hundred meters into a goods yard and stopped. No explanation. He closed his eyes and reflected on the past three days.

His meeting with A.P., Avril Parker, the wife of the oil baron, proved to be very interesting. She, he established, was just as wealthy as her husband, an oversight in his preparations for which he had admonished himself. Though she had been quiet during the dinner, now she showed her strength of character and informed him that she wanted something that no one else in Texas would have. It had to be by a famous artist and be pleasing to the eye. He negotiated a ten percent fee and said he would be in touch when he had the right picture to offer her.

At lunch the Earl, Spencer Harcourt-Smyth, had joined him. "Call me Spence." Always on the lookout to enhance the family collection, he agreed terms and Eduardo said he would be in touch should the right piece became available.

Eduardo opened his eyes at the sound of the train starting to move forward, a cheer worked its way from the front of the train as each carriage picked up the slack in its connecting linkage and started forward. He closed his eyes again as the carriage settled in to a rhythm over the track. In two hours, with luck he would be in a hotel room.

The previous afternoon he had taken to the promenade deck. After ambling around one full turn, he paused at the rail watching the wake of the ship as it receded into the distance.

"There's something about you I do not like!"

Eduardo looked to his left to see the banker standing next to him. George Adams smiled at him.

"Sir, we can not like everybody we meet."

Eduardo looked back at the wake.

"My wife thinks you are very knowledgeable about your particular market."

Eduardo looked back at the banker.

"Your wife is very perceptive. I have a great passion for the arts and I am lucky to be able to earn a modest living through my passion."

"My wife would like you to look out for a painting for her"

"And what would you like, Sir?"

"For you to do what my wife wants."

"You need to keep her happy."

"Sir I want my wife to be happy and if this amuses her so be it. But be warned I will not be duped by you."

"You do not trust people easily, but I have my reputation to think of and a lot of my business is by referral, so it is not in my interest to dupe anybody."

They agreed terms and Eduardo said he would be in contact.

The final surprise came as they came into port at Liverpool. Standing at the rail watching the deck hands secure the ship to the dock he felt that someone was standing next to him, he looked around.

"Good day to you both, have you enjoyed the voyage?"

"Yes thank you, we found it very recuperative."

There stood Hans and Lotti Teidermar.

Hans produced a card and offered it to Eduardo.

"Should you come across an interesting work of art that you think may be of interest to us please contact me."

"May I have a budget that would be agreeable to you?"

"Sir if a piece of art is worth it, I will pay it. Please have a safe onward journey."

"And to you both. Good day."

By the time Eduardo had got to "Good day" both husband and wife had disappeared into the throng. Definitely not ones for small talk!

The train gave him a jolt as it crossed some points. He had been on the move since the ship had docked in the north west of England, but at least once he was away from the ship he could relax. Drop the pretence, remove the glasses and stand up straight. Now he could concentrate on the next phase of his plan. It will be necessary to tell Yves of his plan because he in turn will have to make his preparations, obtain the materials that he will need. So far, he had followed Eduardo's lead without question but he will be impatient to get started. This will take time. Eduardo needed to make contacts. Approaching the wrong person could be fatal to the plan. Eduardo would meet Yves in Montmartre for lunch tomorrow as arranged and go through the plan. They will talk about the time the plan will take to execute once a contact has been made. Eduardo thought six months minimum but Yves never failed to amaze him with the speed he worked. This time a copy would not be good enough. This was the most recognizable painting in the world. It had to be replicated and not just copied.

The train slowed and came to a stop. Everybody gathered their possessions and gratefully left the train. Eduardo had no accommodation but knew there would be hotels close to the station. He would book in for two nights and give himself time to find his way around the city. Once he had a target he would stay closer and build a relationship with the target. For tonight he would be happy with a meal, a glass of wine and then sleep.

CHAPTER THREE
THE PLAN

Eduardo emptied the remains of the wine bottle between their two glasses. They had met as planned and spent their time over lunch regaling each other with tales of their crossings from America.

Yves sighed, "Ok, what is it I am going to paint?"

Eduardo smiled, "The Mona Lisa"

Yves laughed, "Eduardo, you are mad!"

"So you can't paint it?"

Yves coloured up.

"I can paint anything, but there is no point because it is in the Louvre."

"At the moment"

Eduardo had a twinkle in his eye.

"Yves, we are going to find someone to steal it for us"

"Who?"

"Well, we need a dissatisfied worker that we can manipulate."

"How are you going to find this person?"

"I won't. You will."

"I paint,. You do the other stuff, and it's always worked that way."

"All I need you to do is give me a target"

"How?"

"Get a job as a conservator or restorer, they will recognize your talents and take you on, then just talk to people. Once you find someone give me as much detail as you can and I will do the rest. But at no time will we both meet with this person at the same time."

"Ok I can do that."

"It will also give you a chance to look at the painting in advance."

"I only need the real dimensions, I already know the techniques."

"What about raw materials, canvass and paints?"

Yves laughed.

"Not canvass, wood. Not paints, glazes."

"Ok. So I know nothing about how Da Vinci painted, but I will learn."

"You had better know more than the people you are selling to!"

Eduardo looked at Yves

"How authentic can you make the copies?"

"I can start practising now on a technique called sfumato which produces the smoky, hazy look of the painting, blurring all the lines. The difficulty is the ageing."

"What can you do about that?"

"Well the painting is three hundred years old, so I have to affect the finished work to create the craquelure pattern on the surface of the painting."

"You mean the dried out look you get on old Masters?"

"That's right but I have to create the same size and structure or a reasonable expert will see it as a fake"

Yves took a sip of his coffee.

"Eduardo, how many copies do you require?"

"Six would be good. Can you do it?"

"Yes, I can paint them at the same time and replicate each stage. The problem comes with the ageing process. That is the tricky part. I think I had better start with ten to account for problems."

"How long will you need the painting for?"

"Two days at the most for measurements and tonal references."

"I want it in our hands for as little time as possible. Now finish your coffee, for I feel it is time to go and see this new lady in our lives."

They looked at it. Despite being jostled by the throngs of people they maintained their position.

Eduardo spoke out of the corner of his mouth.

"Its smaller than I thought it would be!"

Yves chuckled.

"It's big enough to be painted on a plank of wood and not too big to carry."

Eduardo smiled.

"Point taken! I do not like the glass box they have put it in."

"They must be afraid of vandals."

They moved to look at the other works in the Salon Carre, noting the guard and the locked doors in the corner of the room. Then they moved on through gallery after gallery, room after room in the museum.

Eduardo shook his head

"I can't believe the size of this place. I wonder how many people work here."

"Must be hundreds, cleaners, guards, conservators, guides, historians."

"They must each only know twenty or thirty people. That means if you know your way around and have the right papers you could walk anywhere."

They walked out into the fading light of the evening and stopped at a café with a view overlooking what they believed to be the workers entrance. They ordered wine and Eduardo took out a small notebook.

"So our actions for tomorrow are as follows. You must approach that door over there and see if they are looking for artists to help with restorations. You must also draw up a list of your requirements and I will start to acquire them."

"Well, you can start by finding some wood. Poplar wood as old as you can get."

"And where do you propose I will find such wood?"

"Old panelling, shutters, that sort of thing. The older the more stable it will be, as long as there is no rot."

"Well Yves, I think you may have the easier job tomorrow."

"That's because I have all the talent!"

They both laughed because Yves never took his artistic gifts too seriously.

The arrangement was to meet at six thirty the following evening. Eduardo arrived at the café first. It was a fine July evening so he took a table outside. The waiter appeared and he ordered a bottle of wine and two glasses, declining the menu until Yves arrived.

Eduardo spied Yves bustling up the street looking distinctly put out. He saw Eduardo and made a beeline for his table, sat down and poured himself a glass of wine, which he drank in one tilt of his elbow.

"Well good evening to you Yves!"

Yves, still catching his breath from his walk, mumbled.

"Evening"

"Whatever is the matter?"

"I got a job at the Louvre!"

"That was quick! I thought it would take a week or two for you to do that."

"As a painter, Eduardo, a painter."

"Well, that's perfect!"

Yves was shaking his head and looking more miserable

"No Eduardo, as a painter and decorator."

The laughter started as a low rumble deep inside Eduardo and accelerated to a mighty guffaw so loud that people in the street stopped and stared. This was accompanied by Yves getting redder and redder in the face. Eduardo steadied himself and poured them both some more wine.

"Yves, this is only for a week or two and this way they will not know your real talents."

This went some way to placating Yves.

"They are revising two of the galleries so there is work for a month at the most. A decorator!"

The final two words were spat out with a shake of the head.

Eduardo started to laugh again.

CHAPTER FOUR
THE TARGET

Two weeks passed with Yves working at the museum and Eduardo trying to get the right materials. The most difficult part was the poplar wood that Yves required.

His best chance was to find a very old house and obtain the panelling. After three false dawns, Eduardo finally got hold of over thirty pieces of wood that he thought would be acceptable to Yves. He arranged to have them delivered to the studio and awaited Yves' approval that evening over their evening meal.

Eduardo arrived after Yves and by the smile on Yves face he was happy with the wood.

"Nice to see you smiling for a change! So I presume the wood meets your high standards?"

"Well actually it will do the job once we resize it, but that's not why I am smiling."

"Well why then?"

"I think we have our disenchanted employee."

The waiter approached and they ordered, a little distractedly.

As the waiter walked away Eduardo said.

"Tell me about this person."

"He is an Italian carpenter by the name of Vincenzo Perugia who believes that the Mona Lisa should be in Italy. He believes the painting is a national icon and should be in Rome or Florence. He is well thought of in his occupation and enjoys living in Paris. But I am saving the best piece of information to last."

"What?"

"He is the carpenter that constructed the glass box our lady resides within."

Eduardo's jaw sagged. He took his glass and silently toasted Yves.

"Pure gold Yves, this is better than we could ever have hoped. Now we need to know where he lives."

"Five Rue de l'Hopital-Saint-Louis"

Yves sat there with a very smug expression.

"Well you have been busy! What does he look like?"

"I am meeting him for an aperitif later this evening, so you can follow me and see for yourself."

Eduardo raised his glass again.

"Yves, well done, well done indeed. He must not see us together."

"Yes I know. We can discuss it on the way, drink your wine or we will be late."

They walked over to the St-Louis area of the city and approached the café where they were due to meet.

Eduardo stopped at the street corner.

"It will be best if I go in first. Wait five minutes and then come in."

Yves nodded in agreement and watched as Eduardo did his famous transformation into the scholarly old man he had perfected. He had seen him do this act many times but its effectiveness still amazed him.

Yves entered the café and saw Perugia straight away, standing at the bar. As he approached, Yves spied an old man sitting at a table in the centre of the room talking to the waiter about his menu choice. Perugia looked up as Yves approached the counter. Eduardo could only catch the odd word of the conversation at the counter, but knew it was only pleasantries at this stage. He watched as Yves pointed to the table next to Eduardo's and Perugia nodded his agreement and they made their way over, sat down and viewed the menu. They ordered and started to talk about the internal politics of the Louvre.

Eduardo's food arrived and he started to eat the rich stew of horsemeat. His ears open to the dialogue at the next table. Perugia had a refined moustachioed face, not immediately Italian but once he spoke, his passion in the way he addressed every subject gave his nationality away. Eduardo started to think about who he was to become so he could befriend Perugia and then encourage him to remove the painting from the Louvre.

Eduardo ate his meal and started to formulate a persona for his friendship with Perugia. He would have to appear connected, known in certain business circles, the wrong sort of business circles. Because of his accent and looks he decided to be Spanish, Miguel Torres would do for a name. He would only have to hint at his associations to the underworld to make Perugia feel like a conspirator.

Eduardo left the café and went in search of Perugia's address. Two streets away he found it and moved on to the next street. He found what he was looking for, a room to let sign. Miguel Torres would return in the morning to take up residence. He started his walk across the city to Montmartre, to Yves' studio to await his return.

Eduardo had fallen asleep in a chair and was startled by Yves staggering in the door. Eduardo looked at his watch,

"You took your time."

"That man can drink for Italy!"

"Are you sober enough to have a reasoned conversation or do we wait till tomorrow?"

"I'm fine but you could make some coffee while we talk."

Eduardo shook his head and pushed himself out of his seat.

"Tomorrow we move into the next phase of the plan. I will become Miguel Torres and you will start to work less and less at the Louvre."

"That sounds fine. I have enough to do here with preparation and practice."

"You need to scale back your work slowly so that no one misses you."

"I understand. Miguel, is that the best you could come up with?"

"It doesn't matter really as long as he believes it and I can draw him in to the plan."

Eduardo carried the coffee back from the stove.

"In the morning I will check out of my hotel and then buy some new clothes. I will come here and change into the Miguel clothes and leave my other things here. Then I will go and find accommodation close to Perugia. What time will he finish work?"

"Six"

"Then I will be waiting for him in his local café."

Miguel lent against the bar sipping his pastis, dressed in a second hand suit purchased that morning from the market, good quality but a little shabby, shirt starting to fray at the cuffs. Glancing in the mirror on the wall behind the counter, he could watch for Perugia's approach. He had been there for half an hour when he saw him turn the corner and enter the café. Perugia ordered a pastis and water, watching the clear liquid turn cloudy as he poured the water in his glass. As he took his first drink, Miguel inched his elbow along the counter top causing Perugia to knock it as he put his glass down.

"Sorry."

"No harm done, not a drop spilt."

Miguel nodded towards his glass.

"We enjoy the same poison."

Perugia smiled.

"Probably too much!"

They introduced themselves then went silent for a few minutes. Miguel wanted Perugia to start the conversation, which eventually he did.

"I have not seen you in here before"

"No I came to Paris only yesterday from Madrid."

"Are you looking for work?"

Miguel gave a little laugh.

"No. I have work through the family."

Perugia looked at Miguel and raised an eyebrow. The use of the word "the" and not "my" in Miguel's last response had told Perugia all he needed to know. Born in Italy you understood and asked no questions.

"I work at the Louvre, mostly carpentry, some decorating."

Miguel didn't want the conversation to go in that direction at this stage in their first meeting so left it alone and changed the subject.

"How long have you been in Paris?"

"This is my third year here."

"You like it here?"

"I came for the work. I like the place but the people are rude to outsiders. They think we are stealing their jobs. They never accept you for your qualities as a craftsman. They even call me 'macaroni eater' to my face."

Miguel looked around the establishment, which was filling up for the evening.

"I haven't eaten yet. Will you join me for dinner so I can quiz you about Paris?"

"Sounds like a fair trade to me"

Perugia looked around and nodded towards a table in the corner of the room.

They sat and ordered their food and more to drink.

Perugia asked.

"Did you have a good journey from Madrid"?

"Yes, I stopped in Marseille to visit Family,"

Manuel took the opportunity to reinforce his connection with the criminal underworld.

"But please tell me what I should see while I am here in Paris?"

Perugia talked about the sights and places of interest Miguel should visit while in Paris. Miguel nodding and looking enthusiastic at every place Perugia mentioned. Their food arrived and they ate in silence apart from passing comment on the food, which they agreed was acceptable but lacked Mediterranean flair.

Over coffee and more Pastis Miguel started to lead the conversation in the direction he wanted.

"The Louvre must be an interesting place to work."

"Sometimes, but boring as well."

"All those beautiful works of art to gaze upon every day must be some consolation."

"I have trouble appreciating them when they are not in their rightful place."

"What could be a more fitting place than the Louvre?"

"The country where they were stolen from!"

"I was not aware that the contents were stolen."

"My friend, Napoleon took what he wanted from Europe and I think it should all be given back,"

Perugia's voice had risen causing the other patrons to look in their direction. Miguel gestured for him to lower his voice, which he did to a whisper. Perugia leaning across the table winked at Miguel.

"the Mona Lisa should be in Italy not in the Louvre."

Perugia was now slurring his words.

"Yes but what can you do about it?" Miguel shrugged, "steal it?"

Perugia whispered again.

"I know how to."

Miguel thought, 'this is as far as I want to go tonight'.

"I have had enough for this night. I need my bed."

He called the waiter over and paid the bill.

They left together and went their separate ways at the end of the street agreeing to meet the following night.

Eduardo walked up to Montmartre, finding Yves busy even though the hour was past midnight.

"Well did you meet him?"

"Yes. It went well."

Eduardo proceeded to tell of his first encounter with Perugia.

"So you are pleased with how it is progressing?"

"Yes, it could not have gone better. But I am not the only one to make progress."

Eduardo pointed to the one wall of the loft.

"What is that for?"

A long board had been attached to the wall at a forty-five degree angle.

"Here I will show you."

Yves picked up the pieces of board Eduardo had acquired and put them on the board.

"I call it a running easel. On day one I will start work on the first piece. If it is successful I will replicate that process on the others."

Yves then picked up a rough looking frame from the table.

"But this is the most important piece of apparatus."

He explained that once they have the original painting he would put it in the frame. Around the front edge of the frame is a row of pins, on each pin is a thread with a pencil attached to the end. Then the tip of each pencil will be held above a point on the painting, tip of the nose, or jaw, the thread will be tightened in place. Then when a piece of board is put in the frame an arc can be drawn to indicate the point in question. This will make sure the proportions are correct and will speed the process."

"You are a clever man Yves"

"Yes I know. Of course we need to do the same for the back of the painting."

"I understand. Over the years there will be many marks and references made, we must copy every detail."

"It will all start when we have the exact dimension of the picture. Then we can cut our boards to size and age the back to the same colour."

"Once I have Perugia committed to taking the painting I will ask him. He must know the dimensions after constructing the glass case."

"Well I have done all I can for tonight. Are you staying here or returning to your new accommodation?"

"I will leave you in peace. I want to establish myself in the area so I need to be about for breakfast. I will call by tomorrow, sleep well."

"I will sleep like a baby."

Eduardo left and Yves finished his coffee and made for his bed in the corner of the room.

CHAPTER FIVE
THE PROPOSAL

After two more drunken nights with Perugia, with Miguel stoking the fire of Perugia's sense of injustice, Miguel had decided that this evening he would make the final push to see if Perugia was the man to steal the Mona Lisa.

He decided he would arrive late, and when he did Perugia was already eating.

"My Friend I was beginning to think you were not coming"

"Sorry but business took longer than I thought it would."

"Please sit and order some food."

"Thank you. I am starving. I have had no time to eat today."

This was untrue, as Miguel had slept most of the afternoon. He ordered from the waiter both food and drink for himself and the replenishment of Perugia's glass.

"So what was this business that held you back?"

"I had an idea, a business transaction you might say, and I needed to ask my boss if he wanted to get involved with it."

"What is this idea of yours? It sounds intriguing."

"You have a right to be intrigued because it concerns you."

Perugia's eyes darted around the room but no one was paying them any attention. He knew if it was Miguel's business then it would probably be illegal.

"Let us eat our food first then we can talk business on a full stomach."

Apart from passing comment on the food, they ate in silence. Miguel wanted Perugia sober when he made the proposition so there would be no possible denial tomorrow. The fact that Perugia thought that Miguel worked for the Family, meant that if he said no, he would be too scared to tell a living soul about the proposal. And if he said yes he would have to follow it through for fear of reprisals.

Perugia pushed his plate away while still chewing the last mouthful of his meal. He then had an agonising wait while Miguel finished his food. He dabbed the corners of his mouth with his serviette and draped it across his plate.

"Well my friend, as I said earlier I had an idea which has been approved by the Family."

"Yes?"

Perugia was about to burst with anticipation.

"We would like to help you take a certain painting back to your homeland and become wealthy at the same time."

Perugia's jaw dropped.

"How?" was all he could squeeze out of his throat.

Miguel told him how it would work.

Perugia said he would do it.

"We must see very little of each other in the coming weeks. I will be in this café every night, but you must only join me when you have the painting. Do not bring it with you. We will arrange to meet in plain sight the following day."

"I will try and take it tomorrow."

"Do not rush this. Wait for the right moment and the minimum risk. There will always be another day."

"So wait for the right opportunity?"

"Exactly"

They drank in silence for a few minutes then Miguel asked how he would hide the painting when leaving the museum.

"Under my smock, without the frame it is quite small."

"How big is it?"

"77 by 53 centimetres"

Miguel committed the size to memory.

"Good. So we are in agreement and you are happy with the plan?"

"Yes. Let us have a drink to seal the pact."

They drank for the next two hours, and then Miguel helped Perugia through the door and into the stillness of the Paris night.

CHAPTER SIX
THE THEFT
AUGUST 20TH 1911

He walked the streets for hours.

He could not believe he had done the deed.

He knew why he had done it, out of patriotism and justice, to return the painting to its homeland and the promise of money.

He walked muttering to himself, only pausing to cross himself as he thought of what his sainted mother would think of his actions. He tried to be a good son, sending money to her whenever he could, but the delights of the city often drained his resources. The city of his birth, Dumenza, had driven him to France three years before with the promise of work.

He had struggled from the age of twelve to make a living as a carpenter, the trade given to him by his grandfather. Finally making the journey to Paris where he was told his trade had a market value. Though he was grateful for a living, he hated the fact that he would always be second in line for work behind a Frenchman, regardless of their level of competence when compared to him. This he accepted in the beginning, but now it gnawed away at him.

He had left the Louvre with the painting under his smock, returned to his rooming house and hid it in a trunk. He would see Miguel in the bar tonight and arrange to pass it on to him. He walked on along the banks of the Seine until he had stopped shaking.

He was slowly starting to feel relaxed as he walked back to his lodgings, his hands had stopped shaking and his heart was at its normal tempo.

He spent the early evening in a local cafe waiting for the news to break, but when it didn't, he moved on to the bar to meet Miguel.

"Well I have it" was the thing that came out of his mouth before he had said hello.

"Easy Perugia, there is plenty of time for that. What would you like to drink?"

"Pastis of course. Sorry! Please"

They got their drinks and moved to deserted corner of the establishment.

"Now, all is well?"

"Yes no problem. I had a little trouble getting out of a door I expected to be open which was locked, but I got a plumber to use his key."

"You knew this plumber."

"No but there are so many of us, that he didn't think anything of it. When do you want it?"

"In the morning nine thirty outside here. The street will be busy and we will not be noticed. I will give you a few francs for it, to make it look like a normal transaction."

Miguel finished his drink .

"I will leave now but we will meet here again in two weeks' time to arrange for you to take it back."

"Ok but what am I to do with it then?"

"As we discussed, nothing for two years then whatever you like. Take it back to Florence or Rome."

"And the money?"

"I will look after you. You know the arrangements so be patient. If you leave Paris, leave a forwarding address here and I will be in touch when all is settled." If the painting becomes public again before the two years are up, there will be no money for anyone, do you understand?"

"Yes, I will keep it hidden."

With that Miguel was gone.

Perugia awoke the following morning with a stiff head.

He had grown fond of Pastis in the three years he had lived here but the feeling was not mutual.

He squinted out of his window at the Paris rooftops bathed in sunlight and tried to focus on what he had done the previous day. As a carpenter he worked mainly for the Louvre. Yesterday it was closed for cleaning and maintenance but he and the other carpenters were busy preparing for a new exhibition. It was the fourth straight day he had worked.

So today he was supposed to be off work. This was both good and bad.

He had time to think what he would do next, but he also had time to think about what he had done.

He was ready to meet Miguel by eight thirty, pleased to be getting out of his room and rid of the painting. The blank walls seemed to close in on him with every throb of his head. Save for the picture of Jesus Christ and the cross he had purchased from the flea market the day he arrived in Paris, the place was bare of personal touches.

He was waiting for Miguel on the street corner and had looked at his pocket watch twice already. He felt all eyes were on him, getting progressively paranoid when he saw Miguel stride through the crowded street. He thrust the painting at him and snatched the five-franc note from his hand, turned and walked away. Miguel tried to make casual conversation but as Perugia had already turned and started to disappear into the throng of people he gave up.

Perugia went to the corner cafe and ordered a cafe au lait and a croissant, hoping it would settle his stomach.

He was in a world of his own when he heard a lady at the next table say, "They say it was a master criminal gang who stole it."

He felt relief that the story was out and he had discharged himself of the picture. He had two weeks to figure out what to do with it when he got it back.

Eduardo arrived at Yves' studio after a brisk walk across the city. His heart was racing, his palms sweating.

"Yves I have it."

"Good. We can start real work at last."

Eduardo ripped away the old newspaper covering and passed it to Yves. Yves gave a glance at the picture and then turned it over.

"Don't you want to look at it first?"

"My dear Eduardo I will be heartily sick of looking at it over the next two weeks. First we must reconfirm the size of the board and see if there are any imperfections."

Yves placed the painting face down on a cushion and compared it with one of their pre-cut boards.

"There! See the corner is slightly rounded."

Yves took a file and adjusted the board.

"And here, there is a splinter missing along the grain."

He took a knife and gouged a piece of the wood away.

They repeated the process with all the boards.

"Right. Now the colour"

He went to the sink and returned with a ball of cloth.

"I have saved the old coffee grounds and wrapped them, so we should just be able to rub across the board to get the colour we require."

As he talked he worked the cloth across the board.

"We will see when it dries if I have it right. Now, the inscription and labels."

Yves cut a copy of the labels out of a sheet of paper taken from one of four old books he had bought in the flea market. It was thick and yellowed with age. When he was happy, he passed the labels to Eduardo.

"Your first task. We need twelve of each."

Eduardo nodded and sat down at the table to begin the process. Some of the inscriptions on the board were in pen, some were made with a brush.

Yves had his tools around him and began to copy across, measuring his starting points and working from the top to the bottom. When he was happy, he took the copy labels and produced matching calligraphy.

Within two hours they had completed one board. The labels in place, Yves gave it one last rub with the coffee soaked rag.

"It looks new at the moment but I have some powder that we will dust them with when we have finished all twelve."

They stopped for a hastily prepared lunch and then used their completed board as a template for the remaining eleven. Eduardo shaping the boards, Yves completing them.

By seven that evening they had completed all twelve. Both fatigued by their hours of concentration, they ate a meal of bread and cheese washed down with rough red wine. They ate in silence until all the food was gone then finished the wine. Yves moaned, not completely satisfied with what they had achieved, but he never was happy with his own work.

For the next two weeks, one of them would be in the studio at all times. They had pinned a sheet to the ceiling, hanging down in front in the door, it would deter prying eyes should they open the door and a stranger be passing by.

Eduardo stretched.

"I had better go to my lodgings. I will be back with breakfast in the morning. Yves, don't work all night, you will only get frustrated with yourself."

"I will work on the markers using the frame I showed you, so you can copy the points across tomorrow and I can start painting the background."

"Make sure you bolt the door when I have left."

"Yes papa."

Eduardo gave him an old fashioned look and made for the door.

"Don't do too much."

Eduardo heard, "yes papa" as the door closed behind him, the bolt rasping into place. As Eduardo walked across the city he knew his friend to be a genius and it was a waste not to be creating his own work, but after this he could paint for the rest of his life and not ever have to worry where his next meal was coming from.

But what would he do? His talent was people. To continue with his deceptions will only end with a mistake and prison, so he must find another way to fuel his mind. There would be time for that when this was over. His job for the next two weeks was to protect Yves from himself, let him work, support him but make sure he didn't push himself too far.

CHAPTER SEVEN
THE ROBBERY

Inspector Brunet sat in the museum curator's office looking through statements. They had sequestered the office for the length of the investigation. The heat of the day was beginning to build even with the window open and the fan was making its ridiculous juddering noise above his head.

There was a knock on his office door and his assistant entered with a fresh cup of coffee, replacing the half full cup of cold coffee on his desk and turned to leave.

Brunet looked at it with disdain.

"I need water not coffee."

The assistant went to leave

"Sit down a minute Pierre"

"Yes sir"

Pierre did as he was told. He had been the Inspector's assistant for four years and knew what was coming. Things were not happening quickly enough for his boss.

"How do you think the investigation is going?"

"Sir?"

"I mean, do you think we are proceeding in the right way?"

"Well sir, I don't see what else we could be doing. With sixty investigators on the case, we are sure to get a breakthrough any time."

"Yes, but time is of the essence. The longer it takes, the harder it will get."

"With six hundred employees to eliminate from the inquiry and forty nine acres of museum to search, it will take time. We are still waiting for that scientist Bertillon to come back with his findings on the finger print he found on the frame."

The frame had been left in a stairwell next to the Salon Carre.

"Pierre, we are missing something. This is either a meticulously planned operation or a pure opportunist and until we determine which, we can not move forward."

"We have heard nothing from our contacts in the underworld?"

"No Pierre not yet, which is strange. Usually somebody wants to make himself look good by spouting forth in a bar or cafe about what his boss is up to."

"Inside job then?"

"Pierre whether or not this is a master plan or an opportunist thief, knowledge is the key. So yes somebody working at the Louvre knows about the theft.

I had better start interviewing the main witnesses, send in the painter."

"Yes sir, right away."

Pierre stopped in the doorway

"Drink while it is warm." Nodding towards the coffee on the desk.

"Being the mother hen does not suit you Pierre!"

Pierre coloured up and left the office.

Brunet shook his head and pulled the painter's statement from the pile in front of him.

Louis Beroud, Painter,

Objecting to the Mona Lisa being encased in a glass frame, he intended to paint a portrait of a woman putting on lipstick in the reflection of the glass, thereby making a statement about how the glass detracted from the painting.

When he arrived, the painting was not there and he was annoyed because he had made an appointment and paid the woman to model for him and the light was right to capture her reflection.

He asked the guard to call the attendant. He duly arrived and said that the picture was probably being photographed, as this was happening to all the works of art. He went to find out and came back saying that it was not in the studio. He called the director who was at home. He knew of no reason that the painting should not be in its rightful place. Then the police were called.

There was a knock on the door and Pierre showed Beroud in and made the introductions.

"I have given my statement. I can not see what more I can add."

"I will be the judge of that. Please tell me in your own words what happened."

Beroud then proceeded to give an almost identical account to that which appeared in his statement.

Brunet didn't like him. He was arrogant and pompous with no just cause. But he could not see a reason to detain him, so allowed him to leave.

Pierre returned after showing Beroud out and passed a note to the inspector. Brunet screwed the paper up and threw it at the wall, shaking his head.

"So much for science! Apparently we only keep right handed prints on file and the print on the discarded frame was from the left hand, so it is useless."

He sat with his head in his hands.

"We need to interview all the staff that came into contact with the painting in the last month, search their homes and their bank accounts."

"Yes sir"

"Draw up a list. We will start with the photographer. Where is he?"

"I believe he is in his studio"

"I will pay him a visit myself, now"

"Will I accompany you?"

"No Pierre, finish the list and make sure you have their home addresses. We will see them this afternoon."

With that Brunet left the office and Pierre busied himself on the phone speaking to the managers of every department.

Brunet entered the the photographer's studio.

"Shut the door. Did you not see the notice not to enter?"

"I did but I chose to ignore it."

"Then you can stay where you are and I will get security to remove you from the building."

More arrogance! Brunet was becoming weary of the people in this museum.

"You are Hugo Rogue?"

"I am, and you are?"

"Inspecter Brunet"

"So, you look for the Mona Lisa?"

"I have some questions, if you have some time in your busy day."

Brunet was playing with this idiot.

Rogue looked up from his desk.

"Perhaps next week."

"Hugo Rogue, I arrest you for obstructing my investigation."

Rogue looked up from his desk in shock then smiled.

"You are not serious Inspector."

"I take my work very seriously Mr Rogue. Shall we go?"

Brunet gestured towards the door

"There is no need for this Inspector, I can answer your questions here, now."

"I am glad you are able to find the time."

Rogue stood from his desk and approached the inspector, extended his hand with a slight nod of his head.

"At your service Inspector."

"Very well, Monsieur Rogue."

Brunet referred to the personnel file in his hand.

Hugo Rogue was thirty two years old and regarded as at the forefront of modern photography. He had worked at the museum for just over two years. He had studied art before turning to the camera.

"When did you last see the Mona Lisa?"

"Two weeks ago."

"And why was that?"

" I have developed a way of photographing paintings in great detail, showing every crack in the paint, every imperfection. This is what I did two weeks ago, and this is what I am doing for most of the paintings in the collection."

"What is the point of doing this?"

"They will be photographed again in two or three years and we can see if they have deteriorated. Also, if you find the Mona Lisa we will be able to determine if it is real or fake."

"When we find the painting, I will bear that in mind."

"Would you like to see the the results, Inspector?"

"That will not be nessesary at this time. You handled the painting yourself?"

"The procedure is for the painting to be brought here by a guard and a conservator, I take the photographs, then it is returned."

"Monsieur Rogue, thank you for giving your time freely, my sergeant will inform you if we need your further assistance."

Brunet left the studio without further words. He would not be visiting any more of the suspects, they would be summoned to his office at a given time.

On returning to his office he found a list on his desk.

Guard

Restorer

Cleaner

Carpenter

Maintenance

Underneath the list were a stack of personnel files.

Brunet sat down heavily in his chair and looked at the list to decide which file to start reading, he smiled.

"Pierre"

His sergeant came into view in the doorway.

"Sir?"

"You missed one!"

"Who?"

"The one person who has more access than all of these put together."

Pierre smiled.

"The head of security?"

"Correct."

"I will get his file right away."

"And some water Pierre, don't forget the water."

CHAPTER EIGHT
TECHNIQUE

Eduardo knocked on the door and waited. He had picked up croissants on his way and hoped Yves had the coffee pot on the stove. After banging three times, Eduardo heard the key turn in the lock and the bolt he had fitted slide back with a rasp. The door creaked open and Yves' sleepy face peered around the jamb.

"Oh it's you!"

He stepped back and let Eduardo pass through the doorway and then relocked and bolted the door.

"Who else were you expecting?"

"I was asleep. What's the time?"

"Time for croissants and coffee!"

Eduardo held up the ribbon-wrapped parcel of food, then looked worriedly at Yves.

"How long have you been asleep?"

"A few hours maybe, I do not know."

"Yves, you must take enough rest or your work will suffer and you will become frustrated. I will stay here tonight to make sure."

"You do not have to treat me like a child."

With that he walked to the sink and washed his face then reprimed the coffee pot and set it on the stove. He turned to see Eduardo studying the main easel.

"I'm not happy with it."

"You never are, but it looks good to me."

"Good is not good enough. There is no depth to the painting. I have to create more depth."

The coffee started to gurgle in its pot. Yves used a cloth to pick up the pot and brought it across to the table and sat down.

Eduardo opened the package of croissants and offered one to Yves. He took one reluctantly.

"Yves, you are always like this when you start a painting. You put too much pressure on yourself. Remember we could take up to two years to complete the copies."

"My frustration is within me Eduardo, I can not change the way I am."

"I know. It makes you the artist you are, the perfectionist in you drives you forward, but I will not let it affect your health. So when you have finished your coffee, you will go for a walk for thirty minutes."

"I have much to do."

"Yes you do, after you have been for your walk."

Yves smiled and clapped Eduardo on the shoulder.

"Ok, if you are determined to save me from myself, so be it."

"While you are out, you can buy us some lunch."

"And what would you like"?

"I will leave that to you. What can I be doing while you are away?"

"I have drawn an area of the background on all the boards that need to be blocked in with a brown glaze. Apply it thinly and evenly."

"Right. Off you go for your walk."

Yves sighed and made for the door. Eduardo followed and locked the door behind him. Eduardo returned to the main easel. He looked at the painting again and knew why Yves was frustrated. The portion of the picture which was completed was an exact copy of the original but looked new and without feeling, without depth. He had no fear that Yves would find a way to overcome the problem. His job at this time was to look after Yves.

Eduardo worked away at his task with the brown paint not noting how the time had passed. There was an almighty banging on the door, which startled Eduardo.

He ran to the door and asked whom it was.

"It is me! Who else would it be? Now let me in."

Eduardo unbolted the door, which was pushed open before he could move out of the way. Yves pushed some parcels at Eduardo.

"Food. I think I have it!"

Eduardo, knowing it was pointless trying to make sense of what Yves was going on about, put the food on the table and went back and closed and bolted the door.

He turned round to see that Yves had taken his coat off and dropped it on the floor, gone over to the little box where he kept six jars. He removed two, poured liquid from the first into a vial then added a drop from the other, screwed the lid down tight and shook it vigorously. He looked up at Eduardo.

"You see Da Vinci took four years to complete the painting, which was partly due to the way they manufactured their glazes, very thin layer upon layer was used to create the depth of tone. Each layer having to dry before the next one was applied."

Yves looked at the vial in his hand.

"I think this is the right combination, but there is only one way to know."

He walked over to the picture and unscrewed the lid on the jar. Taking a wide flat brush he applied the clear liquid to the picture. The effect was stunning. It seemed to blur all the lines, immediately giving depth to the picture.

"Yves you are a genius!"

"Eduardo you are correct."

Eduardo shook his head.

"I will recharge the coffee pot and see what delights you have brought for lunch."

"Have you finished applying the brown?"

"All but two because somebody hammered on the door"

Yves walked over to inspect the work.

"We will make an artist out of you yet."

"Not in a million years. I know what is good but have no idea how to put it on canvas."

There was silence for a while, and then Eduardo asked the question.

"Yves what is in your six little jars?"

"Smell the painting."

Eduardo raised an eyebrow and walked across to the picture, bent over and took a sniff. He straightened up and looked over at Yves.

"It smells like piss!"

"Yes different animals give out different levels of acid, the art is to get the balance right for the age of the painting and the mix of the pigments. I strongly suggest that you do not sniff all the jars, some would make you ill."

"How do you learn about these methods?"

"You have to remember that up until the last fifty years, painters and artists made their own paints. It was a major part of the training in classical times. They were trained as apothecaries. They had to make use of what was available naturally."

"Yves?"

"Yes"

"Remind me to never ask you how you fill the jars."

"Ask me no secrets and I will tell you no lies."

"Time for coffee."

CHAPTER NINE
QUESTIONS

Brunet sat at his desk awaiting the arrival of the head of security. They had talked several times over the past few days but now he would interview him as a potential thief. Brunet was more tired than he had ever felt in his life. This was a mental condition more than a physical one. Most detectives would give their right arm for a case like this once in their careers but he hated the attention the case was getting and the interference he received from his superiors. Dealing with the politics of the case frustrated him and left him drained.

In the last three days he had interviewed all the people with the opportunity to steal the Mona Lisa and had reached the conclusion that none of them had the intelligence to carry out such an audacious deed.

The photographer was full of conceit but had other distractions in his life, namely his home studio and his pornographic postcard business. That coupled with the fact that he only had the painting for one hour with the guard waiting at the door ruled him out.

Then they established that the regular guard was at home looking after a sick child, which had been verified by doctors. The illness only occurring overnight so could not have been planned. His replacement was guilty of going outside for a cigarette, which was verified as correct by another member of staff who shared the same vice. Brunet was convinced that this was not an opportunist theft so this excluded the guard.

The cleaner of the salon and the maintenance man were husband and wife. Both were middle-aged and of long service to the Louvre. They very rarely worked together and Brunet found them a doting couple with four children to provide for. The only way they would be involved was if they were press-ganged into it. Brunet could see no indication of that in the interview.

The carpenter, an Italian and a hard worker by all reports. Having worked at the Louvre for three years, he sent money back to his family in Italy and spent the rest enjoying the wonders of Paris. He was worried that the painting had been stolen out of the glass box he had built for it and that he would be responsible.

Brunet assured him that no one blamed him for the theft as the box was built to deflect unwanted attention and not to stop a theft. The carpenter said it had been three weeks since he had seen the picture and asked if he would be allowed to repair the damage to the box. Brunet said that would be possible in the following week. That alone sold Brunet on the idea that the carpenter was not involved, believing that he would want to keep his distance from the scene of the crime, had he been involved.

Then there was the restorer, German, in his sixties. He had never worked on the Mona Lisa in his four years at the Louvre. Grey haired, with half moon spectacles, which he continually looked over throughout the interview. He was opinionated in the extreme. He thought the Mona Lisa was overrated. He enjoyed living in Paris but thought people here lacked respect. The Louvre did not hold him with enough regard and he thought the other employees did not work hard enough. Brunet sent him away after fifteen minutes because he was giving him a headache with his moaning.

Brunet looked up from his desk as the head of security, Martan was shown in by Pierre. Sixty years old. He had held the position for five years after a long and distinguished career in the police.

"Please take a seat"

"Thank you. I take it I am here as a suspect and not a colleague?"

"I am afraid to say you are correct"

"Then am I to assume that you have eliminated all your primary suspects?"

"I think it is I who will ask the questions at this interview."

"As you wish"

They proceeded through Martan's statement. There were no deviations from it in Martan's verbal account of events. Brunet didn't think there would be. The man opposite him had interviewed thousands of suspects himself and knew how to respond whether guilty or not. He would take him past the point of being defensive in his responses by treating him as colleague. Firstly he called in Pierre and arranged coffee to be brought for them.

"I am sorry to put you through this but it has to be done."

"I understand. It is procedure."

The coffee arrived. Brunet dismissed Pierre and they helped themselves.

"So Inspector, have you come to any conclusions about the case?"

"Some but I would be interested to hear your thoughts."

"Well there is obviously inside knowledge of the Louvre and its workings."

"Yes I agree. But what do you do with the most famous painting in the world?"

"There has to be a purchaser for the goods but who would want to own a painting that they could not display?"

"Only the very rich are stupid enough to buy stolen art work that they could not display and lock it away."

"So we have a potential purchaser, the very rich, an inside man who knows the Louvre, but what do we have in between?"

"We agree that this is no opportunist theft. Organised crime would only steal something like this to order."

"Then we have a well planned caper."

"That we do, Monsieur Martan."

Brunet thanked him for his time and said he would keep him informed of any developments. Martan stopped as he opened the door to leave and turned back to Brunet.

"You know we now have a line of people coming to look at the empty space where the painting used to be."

"That does not surprise me!"

Martan shrugged his shoulders and left.

CHAPTER TEN
TWO STEPS FORWARD, ONE STEP BACK

Eduardo settled in to a routine as little more than housekeeper and guardian to Yves, trying to keep Yves on an even keel, even though he swung from elation to despondency and back again with every stroke of his brush. Watching him work was like watching someone solve a great puzzle where all the clues were buried in time.

For the next two weeks, the days blended into one with the routine unaltered.

Eduardo leaving for his rooming house after getting Yves to promise not to pick up his brushes again that evening. The problem was that if it was going well, Yves wanted to carry on into the night and if things were going badly he wouldn't rest until the problem was solved. Eduardo was under no elusion that as soon as Yves had bolted the door behind him, he was back at his work.

Many mornings Eduardo would arrive with breakfast and see that Yves had slept in the chair all night. After the first week he gave up admonishing him. After breakfast Yves was sent on his walk, and always went grudgingly. He would return with some food for lunch which after the first week showed the lack of interest in his chore by the repetition of the same ingredients, namely bread and cheese. Eduardo ended up giving him a list of purchases he was required to obtain. This in turn insured that Yves walked a reasonable distance.

They squabbled like a married couple, bickering back and forth as Yves reproduced the same brush stroke on every painting and Eduardo cleaned and tidied around him. As they sat and ate their lunch Eduardo felt there was something he could not take any more.

"Yves, when was the last time you bathed?"

With a mouth full of food came the indignant reply.

"Wash in the sink every morning."

"Well tonight you will stay in a hotel and give yourself a good scrub down in a bath."

"We cannot leave this place unattended."

"I will stay the night and you will book into the first respectable hotel you see and clean yourself up."

"I do not think that is necessary!"

"That my dear friend is because you do not sit where I do! You will feel better for the experience."

"You make it sound like I never took a bath in my life before and I resent your tone."

"And I resent the smell so as your friend, do it for me."

"As your friend, I will do as you wish."

"Good, I will pack you a bag of clean clothes to take with you."

"Yes mother!"

They both laughed and finished their food.

On his way to the hotel he had stopped for a haircut and shave. Then on to the hotel where he had a leisurely bath and then dressed in his clean clothes before proceeding to a nearby restaurant where he partook his first full meal in almost three weeks. Throughout this process, he never stopped thinking about his painting and what was left to do, the face. Ask an expert to name four features in the background of the painting and they would struggle. The lake, the track, the bridge over the river. Even the chair she sits in and the stone balustrade fade in to the background.

But even to the rank amateur that face had to be the most recognisable portion of any painting in the world. That smile, he didn't like it, but admired the way the artist had created a question that no one could answer. What is her expression?

He was now reduced to eight paintings, which he thought right at this point in the process, four having been discarded along the way when his mistakes became unretrievable. They had cut the boards up and used them as kindling in the stove. The smell of one of the burning boards drove them out of the place, this was to do with Yves applying something from his little box of tricks to try and resolve a problem. They stood outside coughing and spitting the taste out of their mouths for a full five minutes, venturing back in to open the windows, the residue in the air stinging their eyes.

"In all that's mighty Yves, what was that?"

"If we had let it dry out before we put in the stove this would not have happened"

"Are you going to tell me what it was?"

"Are you sure you want to know?"

Eduardo decided that he would sleep easier not knowing.

Yves returned the following morning looking quite the dandy. Eduardo opened the door for him to enter.

"Well you look rejuvenated."

"I am, and thank you for insisting I take this little holiday."

"You needed time away. Did you forget breakfast?"

"No it was most enjoyable. I thought you might like to take a stroll, breakfast and purchase lunch."

"Good idea some air will do me good."

With that Eduardo left and Yves sat in front of the most completed picture. This was probably his biggest challenge and one that he had been playing down with Eduardo. He knew he could do it. The question was how long it would take him to perfect the first face. He uncovered the original and began to study it. That smile. The wisp of a translucent veil across her forehead. The depth of her eyes. Yves knew this was the time to hold himself back, use restraint. But all inside him wanted to race to be finished.

He sat back and smiled, shook his head and started to chuckle to himself as an idea formulated. It brightened his mood for the task ahead.

He said to himself.

"Yves you are very very bad, but it will be so good when it works."

He laughed out loud.

CHAPTER ELEVEN
COMPLETION

The next two days passed with Yves being totally focused on his work and Eduardo looking after him. Eduardo was itching to see a finished painting and he was rewarded early evening on the second day.

"Eduardo could I have your opinion?"

Eduardo looked up from the paper he was reading and smiled. Peering over Yves' shoulder he looked at two paintings side by side. Eduardo came close to tears as his emotions welled up inside him.

"You have such a special talent Yves, the world should know."

"We both know that must never happen and I am happy to be unknown."

"I have to ask you which is the original?"

"On the left. The one on the right is still wet."

"When can I return the painting to Perugia?"

"Tomorrow night, to give this one time to dry overnight and make sure nothing has changed in its tonal quality."

"I will meet him tonight to arrange for him to take it back."

"And the others, how long for completion?"

"How many do you want to start with?"

"One for Austria first. Then two for London"

"You can make plans for Austria now, then one more week for the London paintings."

Yves looked downcast. Eduardo had seen it all before. For Yves the puzzle was solved and the adventure was over. Now it was just a case of replicating his process with the other painting, in which he had no real interest. Eduardo put his hand on Yves' shoulder and gave it a squeeze.

"It will all be over within two weeks, my friend and we can start a new chapter in our lives."

That evening Eduardo put on the shabby suit he had purchased from the flea market and became Miguel again and made his way for his rendezvous with Perugia.

Miguel met Perugia to arrange to see him the following night to exchange the painting. Perugia had had his rooms searched the previous week and had build a small trunk with a false bottom to hide the painting. He seemed a lot more relaxed about the whole affair, which pleased Miguel.

They talked about payment and Miguel schooled him in how and where his money would be available. At first Perugia was sceptical but Miguel convinced him that it would be the safest way to make sure the authorities could not take it away from him, should the police find out his involvement.

The following morning Eduardo booked his passage by train to Austria. He had sent a message to Hans Teidermar the previous evening and was told by reply to arrive at his earliest convenience. He then went to his accommodation and packed his belongings. Leaving the landlady a week's money for her trouble, he made his way to Yves' studio. He had decided to spend the next two nights with his friend. They had been through a lot together over the years and although Yves had not said what he intended for his future, Eduardo knew he would not come back with him to Argentina. The next three weeks will be hectic and they would be seeing each other only fleetingly.

Miguel arrived to find Perugia seated at a table in the corner of the restaurant.

The painting, concealed in a Hessian bag, was placed on the floor against the leg of the table while they ate their meal. Perugia relaxed while they enjoyed the food. Only when it was time to pay their dues and leave did beads of sweat appear on his upper lip. Miguel promised to see him as soon as possible with the details he would need. They arose from the table, Perugia picking up the bag as if it belonged to him. Only the rising colour on his neck giving him away.

They parted with a handshake.

CHAPTER TWELVE
AUSTRIA

Eduardo had arrived late the previous evening. He had changed trains for the last time in Vienna and alighted one hour later at a small rural station. He was the only person to leave the train and as he walked to the end of the platform, a pony and trap pulled to a halt. As there was no one else about he knew the transport was for him. He put his bag in the rear and pulled himself up next to the driver. Neither he nor the driver spoke on the short trip to his destination. The manor house was imposing and showed no signs of life. The retainer showed him to his room and spoke for the first time telling him that breakfast was at 6.30 am sharp. No offer of a drink or food after his long journey. The room was cold and draughty. His only comfort was that he would be away from this place by tomorrow lunchtime and on his way back to Paris.

He arrived at the appointed time for breakfast and was met by Hans Teidermar.

They exchanged a formal greeting and Eduardo was offered a seat at the table across from Hans.

"I hope you slept well."

"Yes thank you."

Eduardo lied, he had shivered the whole night.

This was the difficult transaction and the reason he had come to Austria first. These were the most uncompromising people he would be dealing with. They appeared to have little ego that he could manipulate. If they wanted the painting they would buy it, if not he feared that they might just call the authorities and have him arrested. He knew the line he would take and convinced himself that it would work. For if he himself was not convinced then he could not convince Hans and Lotti Teidermar.

"So Eduardo you think you may have something of interest to us?"

"I feel I may, but before I tell you about it I feel I must explain why I have brought it for you to see and not one of my other clients."

Hans left eyebrow rose with interest.

"Please do not create intrigue to try and embellish the sale. It will not work with me."

"I will speak only in fact and you can be the judge as to my sincerity. Two weeks ago I was referred to a new client by an old acquaintance in Paris. At the time I thought it strange that this person would refer someone and not ask for a percentage of any transaction when it was completed, but then put it out of my head and duly went to the meeting, which was in a hotel room.

Two men were present and they informed me that they had a painting for sale. These people did not look like art dealers and I became uncomfortable in the situation. They said that they had had a buyer for the painting but the person changed their mind at the last minute so they were left with the painting on their hands and just wanted to get what they could for it. They then showed me the painting. I was astonished and said I could not help them. They assured me that I would help them or there would be grave consequences."

Hans moved a little in his chair.

"You did not go to the police?"

"I feared that it would be the end of me if I approached the authorities. These people have long arms."

"So why are you bringing your trouble to me?"

"I bring you no trouble. This is my problem and mine alone. The reason that I have come to you is because you will look upon this as an opportunity to own a Master with the discretion required not to show it off to all and sundry.

"Please Eduardo show me this painting."

So he did.

"Now I understand."

"It is a painting that is difficult to look away from once you look at that smile."

"It is genuine?"

"From when it was taken till I first viewed it was five days and no one could copy the Mona Lisa in that time."

Eduardo turned over the painting showing the labels and markings.

"As you can see there is much documentation on the back."

Hans raised his head for the first time since the painting had been uncovered.

"Now I understand why you brought it to me. Most of your customers would not be able to resist showing it."

"That was my fear."

Hans lent forward and turned the painting over, studying it, hoping it would tell him something. He then spoke without looking up.

"How much will it cost me?"

"Five hundred thousand American dollars."

Hans smiled, still not looking up from the painting.

"A heavy price for a stolen painting that your clients want off their hands!"

"I can negotiate a little on behalf of these people but I would not like to think of them as my clients. I want rid of the whole affair."

They negotiated to three hundred thousand and Hans said the money would be in a bank of his choosing by the end of the week. Eduardo stressed the buyer of the painting would not be divulged to the sellers unless payment was not forthcoming, at which time Hans would be contacted directly. Hans assured him that it would be a straight transaction.

Eduardo left before lunch feeling happy with himself. Now he could pay off Perugia and close that chapter of the affair.

CHAPTER THIRTEEN
ONE DOWN

Eduardo arrived back in Paris exhausted from his trip, having had no sleep for over twenty-four hours. He seemed to have spent as much time stationary waiting for his connecting train as he did on the move. Arriving at the studio he found Yves in a good mood, charging the coffee pot as soon as he arrived and wanting to hear of his adventure into Austria.

Eduardo related the details as he sipped his coffee, the caffeine having no effect on his weary body. He finally fell asleep and slept for three hours.

He awoke not knowing where he was or what day of the week it was. Yves laughed on seeing the crumpled state of his friend.

"Why don't you stay the night in that hotel I went to, you will feel better in the morning and I won't have to hear your snoring and look at your craggy face."

"It is nice to know you care about me."

"I mean it. Go book yourself in and take a bath. You will feel better for it."

Eduardo rose from his chair and made for the door.

"I will be back in an hour or two with some food. Bolt the door behind me."

"Yes, o grumpy one."

Eduardo bag in hand, heard the bolt slam shut behind him. He wondered if his tiredness made Yves seem more cheerful than his usual lugubrious self. Or was there more to it?

Eduardo returned later that day with food and a bottle of wine. They enjoyed the meal together. Eduardo, still not understanding why Yves was in a cheerful mood, pressed Yves for an explanation.

"So why are you in this agreeable mood? Is there a woman you are not telling me about?"

"I only have eyes for one woman. She tried to break my spirit but she did not succeed. My talent prevailed."

They both looked across at the easel and smiled.

"Will you be ready for me to go to London next week?"

"Yes. When will you see Perugia for the last time?"

"I will check to see if the money has been wired from Austria in the morning. If it has I can make the arrangements for the accounts and see him tomorrow night. I will be glad to be rid of him. I feel he is a responsibility I have never been in control of."

"I can understand that. Then it will all be down to you and me to finish what we started."

The following morning Eduardo made his way to the bank. The money had arrived and he felt such relief, only then realising the pressure he had been under. He opened three accounts in a Swiss bank. Depositing two hundred thousand American dollars in one and fifty thousand in each of the others.

He then went to a jeweller and purchased three silver crosses, just large enough to have a row of numbers engraved down the back. He chose a silver crucifix because it could be worn without it drawing attention. He thought that even in these days of high crime, a cross was the least likely thing to be stolen.

He sat at their usual table waiting for Perugia to appear. He had ordered drinks.

The drinks arrived at the same time as Perugia. Perugia smiled at him.

"I did wonder."

"If you would ever see me again?"

"Yes"

"Your faith will be rewarded, but let's order some food then I will explain all.

They ordered and while they waited for their food to arrive, Miguel produced something from his waistcoat pocket.

"This is for you."

Perugia looked down at what had been passed to him in disbelief.

"A silver cross! I already have a gold one. It was my grandfather's. Is this what you give me for my trouble?"

Eduardo smiled

"Faith my friend. Look at the back."

Perugia turned the cross over in his hands and looked up at Eduardo.

"That is your account number at the Swiss National Bank."

"I am sorry for not trusting you."

"We must trust each other or we will both be in trouble. Remember, you cannot touch the account or do anything with the painting for two years. Remember Family. You are Family now and that comes with responsibilities."

Their food arrived and they ate in silence. Eduardo knew there was one burning question Perugia wanted to ask but was afraid to, how much.

"I think I will take it back to Italy, leave it in the museum in Florence."

"You may do as you wish but in two years. It is up to you. My advice would be to think carefully, don't jeopardise your inheritance."

As he said it Eduardo nodded at the cross, which was now round Perugia's neck.

"Ok, how much am I likely to inherit?"

Eduardo raised his glass and looking round to make sure no one was paying attention, then spoke in a whisper.

"Two hundred thousand dollars American."

Perugia went pale.

"That is too much. It will ruin me!"

"Think of your children."

"I have no children."

"Yet."

Perugia smiled.

"I will be a good catch now."

"Yes you will, but you must never admit to anyone how much money you have. It could be dangerous for you. Spend some, save some for a rainy day and keep some for your children. Remember Family."

Miguel had had enough of mentoring this man so he made to leave. Perugia started to panic.

"How do I contact you?"

"You do not contact me. I will contact you after the two years has expired."

Eduardo offered his hand to Perugia who shook it and pulled Eduardo into a hug.

"Thank you for helping me to fulfil my dream."

"It has been a pleasure knowing you."

With that Miguel left the restaurant without looking back.

Eduardo got back to the studio and changed out of the old suit, took it over to the stove and proceeded to feed it into the flames. Yves smiled.

"Glad to be rid of that character?"

"Both Perugia and Miguel Torres."

"The next chapter starts tomorrow?"

"Yes I am booked on the boat train to London at midday."

"How long will you be away?"

"About a week"

"I will have finished the last painting on your return."

Eduardo finished feeding the stove and stood and faced Yves.

"I opened accounts for us today. The number is on the reverse of this crucifix."

He passed the cross to Yves.

"There is fifty thousand American Dollars in the Swiss National Bank in your name. I have the same."

"Thank you."

"Should things go wrong for any reason you can still live quite well many years."

"I will be going south to the coast, maybe Spain. I have heard that the air is so clear, the light so pure, it is a painter's heaven."

"I will be going home but I do not know what I will do with my time."

"You will involve yourself in life. You will not be idle for long."

They passed the evening reminiscing about their first meeting and the way their business had flourished, neither of them expecting it to be their way of life for the next twenty-five years but each expecting the next deal to be the last. Not knowing what lay ahead.

But now the dye was cast and within two weeks their futures would be set for life. They both felt this would be a relief but they would also miss the adventure of the uncertain life together.

The next morning Eduardo readied himself for his trip to London. Yves had packed one of the paintings the night before into the base of Eduardo's bag as it was already dry and now passed the other which Eduardo concealed by an extra piece of fabric that matched the rest of the bag's interior. He said his farewell to Yves. Telling him again that if he had not returned in a week to leave the studio in haste and not look back. Eduardo heard the bolt slide shut and turned away. The boat train would leave in under an hour. As he strode towards the station he started to think about the next two clients, the Earl and the Oil Baron's wife.

CHAPTER FOURTEEN
POWER AND POLITICS

Inspector Brunet studied the headline. The news in the paper did not surprise him and he knew this was just the beginning. The Museum Director, Theophile Homille had been forced to resign. The man had no choice, the pressure was intolerable. The country needed someone to blame and he was the obvious target. A new director would be appointed, no doubt already selected and changes would have to be seen to take place.

He had had several conversations with Martan in his role as head of security and knew that he was expecting to be relieved of his post any day. Brunet expected that today would be the day. He decided to visit him in his third floor office. Martan had always been the one to come to his office, so as the man was about to be shown the door, Brunet would show respect by visiting him.

He arrived not a minute too soon. Martan stood behind his desk sorting papers into files. He looked up and smiled at seeing Brunet stand in the doorway.

"I was on my way to your office to bring you these files. They are of no use to me now."

"So the axe has fallen?"

"Yes, I had a telephone call from Homille last night telling me his final act as Director was to terminate my employment."

"Sounds like a nice person."

"Vindictive more like."

"What will you do now?"

"I had been expecting this so I have been looking at some private work. There are plenty of men in Paris who are worried what their wives are doing, while they are doing what they should not. It will pay well once I am established."

Brunet took the offered files and tucked them under his arm, then extended his hand, which Martan accepted.

"Well good luck and if I can be of any help, please call."

Martan produced a calling card.

"If there is any work you think is appropriate to forward to me, I would appreciate it very much."

Brunet took the card and said a final good-bye and left.

Brunet went down the three flights to his office thinking that he would soon be back at his own desk in the Surete head quarters. Two hundred investigators had started the search for the painting and now in their fourth week only thirty remained. There had not been one lead from their contacts in the Paris underworld. All the main suspects that worked at the museum have continued to keep their daily routine. No one showing signs of coming into money. The investigation had stalled.

Brunet got back to his office to receive a message from Pierre that he was to meet with his commander as soon as possible. Pierre had already called for his car.

The Commander looked up as Brunet was shown into his office.

"Brunet, please be seated. I will not detain you long. As you know, you were entrusted with this case because we thought you could handle the public and political pressure that would follow."

Brunet sat and nodded in the appropriate places. He knew what was coming and knew that the commander was not going to enjoy what he was about to do.

The commander continued.

"I think I am fair in saying that in that respect you have conducted yourself admirably."

"Thank you"

"Unfortunately the same can not be said for resolving the case. My superiors want changes and results and I am powerless to resist. Can you offer me any progress to report?"

"No Sir. We keep eliminating people from our enquiries but we have not one lead of substance at this time."

"Then you give me no option but to remove you from the case."

"I understand sir and will cooperate fully with my replacement."

"Please empty your desk at the Louvre and return here to await your next assignment."

Brunet left without saying a word. He knew arguing his case would be futile. He had not achieved the basic requirement of his assignment, to get the Mona Lisa back in the Louvre. He had resigned himself to that fact within a week of the start of the investigation. Not one concrete clue to follow. When you draw a blank so early in a case you know you will struggle.

It would not enhance his reputation but that would be something he would have to live with. He was young enough to ride out the storm. He wondered who would take his place. He did not envy them. He looked forward to a more straightforward case and hoped that there would be one awaiting him on his return.

CHAPTER FIFTEEN
THE PRODIGAL RETURNS

Eduardo hammered on the door to make himself heard over the din that came from inside. Eventually the door opened to reveal a dusty Yves.

"So you are back."

"Yes. What are you doing?"

Eduardo pushed past Yves into the studio. It appeared that Yves was taking apart the long sloping easel he had built along the one wall.

"I thought we had better leave the place as we found it. You can grab that brush and start sweeping up."

"I think I will have some coffee first."

Eduardo put his bag down behind the door.

Yves picked up a hammer and continued to demolish the woodwork.

"Are you not going to ask me how it went in London?"

"You are back a day or two early so I presume it went very well or very badly."

"Well you were right with your first assumption."

"You can tell me all about it this evening."

"I presume you have finished the last painting."

"Yes this morning, it will be dry by this evening and we can be out of this place. I thought we would both stay at that hotel we used before, tonight and have a last meal together."

"Hopefully the money has been wired through to the bank."

Eduardo finished his coffee and took off his jacket, picked up the brush and started to sweep up.

That evening over their meal, Eduardo related his trip to London. His meeting with the Earl and the oil baroness went very smoothly. Both bought into his explanation about being coerced into selling the painting. Eduardo was amused by the fact that while the Earl was looking at the painting, he had another copy in the bag at his feet. He felt like saying, "if you do not like that one, I have another I can show you."

He had booked a passage to America the following day and would take the final painting with him. The Wall St banker awaited his call on arrival. He did not like Adams and Adams didn't like him so their meeting would be straight and to the point. The man's vanity would be the key to this sale. From there he would go back to Argentina.

Yves wanted to paint without having to worry about money and now he could do just that. He would still live simply as he had never been one for possessions apart from his paints and brushes.

Eduardo's trip across the Atlantic was uneventful. On arrival in New York he was asked by the customs officer if he had anything to declare.

"Yes, I have the Mona Lisa in my bag."

The officer laughed and let him through. Eduardo always believed in telling the truth.

CHAPTER SIXTEEN
FORTY-EIGHTH MONTH

Perugia crossed out the final square on his homemade calendar. He had felt in limbo for the past two years, waiting to start his life again. Apart from once taking it out of his trunk to look at it, it had remained sealed in the hidden compartment he had created in the base of the trunk.

Having spent the last two years trying to decide what to do with the painting and coming to no firm conclusion, he had looked upon an advert in the paper the previous week as a divine message. An art dealer in Florence stated that he was looking for works of art for an exhibition. Perugia contacted the dealer and had arranged to meet him in Florence.

He had packed his belongings into the trunk. Looking around the room one last time he pulled the calendar of the wall tore it into small pieces and put them in his pocket. He had slowly reduced the hours he was working at the Louvre over the last two months. He was sure he would not be missed. He lifted the trunk on to his shoulder and left his old life behind.

Perugia had arrived at the Hotel Tripoli-Italia in Florence the previous afternoon.

He had contacted the art dealer, Alfredo Geri and now awaited his arrival to discuss the painting. Perugia thought the man would be happy to see the painting returned to Italian soil but he was very business-like and insisted on taking the painting to have it authenticated. Perugia felt that his part was over and he would be rid of his millstone.

The police arrived and arrested him. He was shocked but not surprised as this was one of the outcomes he had foreseen over the last two years. Truth was that even in the hands of the police he felt safe because he was in his home country.

Eduardo opened the letter from Yves. This was their first communication since he had returned to Argentina

'Eduardo,

I hope this letter finds you well.

I have settled in a fishing village just north of Barcelona, (see address).

I have just read that Perugia has been arrested therefore I feel I have to come clean about the painting that you gave him. It was a copy. My vanity got the better of me, I am afraid. The outcome of this is that one of your clients has the original. To be fair to all I will never say which one has it. I hope you forgive me.

Are you engaged in life? I am sure you are. Please write and tell me.

Sorry if I have disappointed you.

Your Friend

Yves.'

'Yves,

I have just stopped laughing so I can reply to your letter. You never cease to amaze me. This of course could be good news for one of our clients. I am contemplating writing to inform them of the news, before they destroy their painting in a fit of pique after hearing that the 'original' is to be returned to the Louvre. I read that Perugia is to stand trial in Italy, and that he is being looked upon as a national hero. Such is life!

I have purchased a small manor house and have got involved in local issues. This, I am sure, is no surprise to you, but the area has long been neglected by the regional government and I feel I may be able to change that view.

Since starting this letter I have decided to write to our clients and have arranged for the letters to be posted in New York. I have enclosed a copy for your interest.

Please write and tell me of your life in Spain and your painting.

Your friend

Eduardo.

Enclosures:

I am writing with reference to your purchase of a certain painting two years ago.

Four persons purchased the painting, which was produced from the original by probably the most talented living artist of the day. The artist has recently informed me that the original is <u>not</u> the painting being returned to the Louvre. This means you have a one in four chance that your painting is the genuine article. You will hear that the Louvre have ways of knowing that theirs is the original but it is not true. Please be assured that this letter is sent in good faith and while you were misled in your original purchase, the artist and myself hope that this would offer some solace.

Yours with honourable intentions.

Perugia was convicted and sentenced to one year and fifteen days for his crime.

He appealed the sentence and served seven months and nine days. Released without any money in his pocket, he hiked back to his home village of Dumenza and was welcomed as a hero.

He served in the army with honour in the First World War. On completing his service he married an Italian girl, and despite his dislike for the French people moved his family to a French village near the Swiss border. He opened a paint store and went on to have a happy and prosperous life.

After many tests on the Mona Lisa, it was deemed to be the original and after a tour for the museums of Italy, it was returned to the Louvre display on the Fourth of January Nineteen Fourteen where it remains to this day.

FOOT NOTE

In Nineteen Thirty One a reporter, Karl Decker released a story that seventeen years earlier he had interviewed one Marques Eduardo de Valfierno. He revealed his involvement in the theft of the Mona Lisa. Decker was asked not to relate the story until Eduardo had died. The story appeared in the Saturday Evening Post.

PART TWO

CHAPTER SEVENTEEN

He had entered by the visitor's entrance, and the musty smell of this place assaulted his nostrils. Standing in the centre of the place always made him feel like being in the stomach of a whale, this place being just as much a living thing.

He was here after receiving a phone call which had interrupted his morning's work of paper plane production. Business was quiet at the moment. From his second floor office above the charity shop he could see the place he now stood in.

The gist of the call was to meet Lily here and all would become clear. The voice on the phone was that of a younger woman.

He knew of Lily by reputation only, and that was as big as the whole city.

Lily would now be in her mid seventies but in her heyday was the most famous prostitute in the city. The City having a barracks on its doorstep for over one hundred years, the oldest profession had always flourished.

What she would want with him, a fledgling PI in a Staffordshire cathedral city, he hadn't a clue. But as he had got through half a ream of paper and it was still only eleven am, the five hundred yard walk from his office would save his sanity and his paper.

It was now spring and he had left the police force the previous summer in a fit of pique. Too much paper work, not enough support and no confidence that if he put someone behind bars that they would not be out on good behaviour with only half their time served. The system was mad.

The message was to meet by one of the private chapels that clung to the side the cathedral. As he approached he saw a well dressed woman in her mid twenties leaning over to speak to a woman sitting on an electric four wheel scooter, the sort that run you over in shopping centres. They both looked up on seeing him approach.

Charlie walked over to them.

The younger one spoke first with an accent he wasn't expecting, not upper class but well bred.

"Charlie Edwards?"

"Yes"

"I'm Zoe and this is my grandmother Lily. She is going to talk to you but I would ask you not to interrupt, as she is not in the best of health and must not get excited. Save your question for later."

Charlie nodded, wondering what he was letting himself in for.

The old lady pointed at him.

"You know who I am then?"

"Yes"

"Reputation is a great thing" she laughed, which ended up as a wheezy cough. Zoe motioned towards her but Lily waved her off.

"I'm ok, I'm ok, let's begin at the beginning"

Charlie could see that she was warming to the task.

"Charlie I have had an interesting life and through it all there has only been one constant, my family. Zoe, her mother and father and James Barker."

Charlie raised an eyebrow at the name because the Barker family were regarded as the local landed gentry.

"He was Lord Lieutenant of Staffordshire when I met him. Through a client, as I think they call them today, I got an invitation to the Hunt Ball, which in the nineteen fifties was the place to be seen. During the night we danced together and just hit it off. Our relationship went from strength to strength. My only fear was that he would find out who I was or that he would ask me to marry him. You see I knew that it would never work, back then the class system was too strong, it would have damaged him and his family.

But as it was events intervened. I fell pregnant with Sheila. He begged me to let him marry me, I told him he couldn't, he asked why. I told him why and he broke down and cried in front of me."

Lily dabbed the corner of her eye with a tissue, Zoe moved towards her, but was waved off.

"He was such a gentleman all his life. Set me up in a flat and paid for everything while I went through the nine months. Sheila was born and he was there. He brought us home from the hospital and popped in to see us as much as he could.

After the first month I made my mind up to tell him not to call again, he had a life to lead and I didn't want him to call on us if he didn't want to."

The tissue came into view again, this time to blow her nose, the noise of which resounded round the cathedral. Charlie looked about but no one seemed to notice. He turned back to Lily.

"In the end we agreed that he would help support her and that I wouldn't take a penny from him. He set up a trust fund for her to go to a private school but when it came to it she hated it. Sheila was bright but not university material, at least not in those days. She had what you would call a middle class childhood and as a teenager in the late sixties was a bit of a hippy. She fell in the end for Teddy. He was an accountant, they married and a year later Sheila fell pregnant with Zoe."

Charlie saw the young woman's neck go red.

"James transferred the trust to Zoe for her education. Only James knew what was in the fund at that time."

Time for a new tissue. Charlie was wondering where this was going and why he was being subjected to it.

"In 2000, Sheila and Teddy were killed in a car accident. By then my condition had been diagnosed and I was living with them up on the hill. Zoe came back from London to look after me."

Charlie had promised not to speak but he was losing his patience.

"Which brings us to why you are here,"

'Finally' thought Charlie.

"James passed away six months ago. He never married. He told me years ago why. He could never marry and not have Sheila as part of his life and he didn't think it would be fair to his bride to have a ready-made daughter. Such a sweet man."

Yes the tissue was out again.

"He had other women in his life but always pulled away before they got too close. Anyway we were called to the reading of the will. Only six people. He gave money to charity. His household retainers were well looked after and there was a niece who didn't look too impressed with what she got. Then there were us two. What we got was a mystery, Charlie, a mystery.

It's about a painting which came into his family in the nineteen twenties.

He had shown me the picture years ago and he called it "The Barker Folly".

In his later life he decided to look into the history of the painting. You see it is a copy of a famous painting, but the more James looked into it the more he thought there was a real chance that it was the genuine article. He established that apart from his, there are three more copies somewhere. He ran out of time before he could find them. Now it's our job to finish what he started. We have to find those other three paintings. To help us we have his papers and a large sum of money. So this is the deal, there is a pot of money we will inherit minus what ever it costs to find the other three owners. We do not get a penny until the other owners are found.

So Charlie, the question is, are you interested in helping us?"

"Well I'm intrigued, but I have some questions."

"Ok."

"Why me?"

"I beg your pardon"

"Why pick on me to contact?"

"Well Charlie many years ago Sheila was trying to make friends after deciding she didn't want to stay at the private school. She had been there long enough to get a plummy accent and got picked on for it. Just one girl befriended her. Her name was April."

"My Mom?"

"Yes that's right. My chest is tightening up with the musty smell in here, I must go. We will call you tomorrow."

Lily turned the key on her electric scooter, gripped the handlebars and stamped on the accelerator.

Charlie said. "But what is the picture?"

But Lily was disappearing up the ramp and through the exit.

Zoe was trying to keep up with her grandmother while balancing on high heels on the uneven floor. She looked over her shoulder and mouthed something to him that looked like morning Lisa.

Charlie walked to the entrance and squinted in the sunlight, muttering to himself as he went.

'Morning Lisa, well it was just still morning but his name wasn't Lisa, what the hell was she saying?'

Charlie started mouthing Morning Lisa to himself as he passed through the old city gateway into Dam Street.

Suddenly he stopped as he got to Minster Pool and shouted 'Mona Lisa'.

CHAPTER EIGHTEEN

They cannot be serious. He got to the market square and stopped, not knowing what to do next. He decided he needed a drink. The Acorn would do the job.

After downing the first half of his pint in one bend of his elbow he sat and thought through what to do next. He pulled out his phone and found Peter's number, pressed dial.

"Peter Jenkins"

"Peter, its Charlie"

"Hi, what are you up to?"

"I'm in the Acorn"

"And you want to buy me a drink!"

"Afraid not, I need to come to you."

"Typical! I'll get the fire going in the boiler house, see you soon."

That was just his turn of phrase. Charlie knew Peter was going to start up his computer. He finished his pint and headed for the door. Peter Jenkins lived in an end terrace house which backed on to Beacon Park. Peter had been Charlie's Chief Inspector in the force. When his wife died suddenly he decided that he couldn't face working for the police and took early retirement.

After six months of moping around he took a free computer course at the university on a whim. He got hooked. While in the police force he always had someone else to do his paperwork so he had never used a PC. This made the experience totally new.

Two years ago he had started a small business plotting people's family trees. Charlie had seen how Peter could use a computer for searches and was impressed by the speed with which he navigated his way around.

Charlie had met him by chance in the Market Square one day and their friendship blossomed. Firstly it was a bit strange, Peter being Charlie's former boss but once they had got past that, they had become firm friends. Now Thursday night was their curry and pint night, exchanging stories about their cases over a masala. As Charlie approached the house he noticed how immaculate the small front garden was maintained. The whole house was always neat as a new pin. Charlie thought this was a carry-over from Peter's national service. The front door was ajar, he knocked as he pushed it open.

"Come on up, but close the door behind you."

Charlie was already on the first tread of the stairs and had to do an about-turn to close the door.

As he entered the small room Peter looked up from the PC.

"So who are we looking for?"

"It's a what - a painting."

"Never done that before. What's it called?"

"Mona Lisa"

Peter had turned back to the computer but on hearing the last piece of information turned round in his chair and crossed his arms.

"OK. What are you talking about?"

"I need the history of the Mona Lisa."

"Why?"

"Because I have been asked to find some copies, so I need to find out if it has ever been stolen."

Peter turned back to the PC.

"Why do I think you are playing with me?"

"Would I do that to you?"

"Given the chance, yes, and enjoy it!"

"I have to decide if I want to take the case by tomorrow morning, so I need to get a feel for whether it's a viable case or not."

"Intriguing"

As they talked, Peter clicked on a search engine and typed in Mona Lisa.

"Mmm, I think I will need to narrow it down a little"

The screen showed over a thousand hits. He typed theft into the command box and waited.

"There we are. 1911, August theft of Mona Lisa from the Louvre."

"Can you tell me how long it was missing?"

"Yes, it says here that the Italian police got it back in December 1913."

"That's over two years. Plenty of time for someone to copy it."

Peter turned to face Charlie.

"Why don't you give me a couple of hours to sift through all this? I will put you a report together."

"Ok, there is someone else I need to speak to. How about I buy you a pint in the Kings Head at Five?"

"Or two"

"OK or two."

With that Charlie left the room and headed down the stairs and through the front door. Peter was immediately engrossed in what he was reading on the computer screen.

Charlie walked back to where he parked his car and pulled his phone out of his pocket at the same time.

"Hi Mom it's me. Can I pop around for a cuppa?"

"Why, what's wrong?"

"There's nothing wrong and I don't like the inference that I only call when there is something wrong."

"Touchy today, aren't we? I'll put the kettle on."

"OK. See you in five minutes."

Charlie closed his phone and opened his car.

His mother lived in a bungalow in a cul-de-sac, the sort of place where every property is individually designed. His father had bought the land in the late nineteen fifties and took two years over having it built. He was a senior partner in a solicitors' firm in the town that could trace its beginnings back over a hundred years. He had worked his way up from clerk to partner then senior partner only to die when he was about to retire.

As he pulled up on the drive the front door opened, his mother standing in the doorway, as she had done so for so many years during his school days.

"Hi"

He kissed his mother on the cheek and went through to the lounge. She followed and passed him his tea.

"Help yourself to a biscuit"

He did.

"So why the visit?"

"You would think I didn't see you at least once a week."

"Exactly. What couldn't wait till the weekend?"

Charlie mowed the lawns on a Saturday morning and did any heavy work about the house. April Edwards had become fearlessly independent since Charlie's father had died but the mower was too powerful for her and though she had tried a smaller mower, the lawn was too big for it.

"OK Mom, there is something I want to ask you."

"I knew it!"

"Do you remember a girl named Sheila from school?"

"Yes I do. We were friends until she died in a car crash. I went to her funeral."

"You knew her mother?"

"Everybody in Lichfield knows Lily."

"I didn't know you knew her."

"Why should you? I know lots of people you don't know about. Anyway, why the interest in Sheila?"

"Well the interest is in Lily. She has asked me to look into some family business and when I asked why she had contacted me, she said it was because of the kindness you had shown Sheila. So I just thought I would check that you knew her."

"She always had to live with what her mother did for a living and not knowing who her father was."

"She knew who her father was"

"Who?"

"Can't say"

"I'm your mother. You can tell me"

"Maybe soon, but not now"

Charlie got up to leave.

"Oh so that's it! You dangle that nugget of information in front of me and then leave. Typical."

"Sorry Mom, I shouldn't have said anything."

"Well I hope this job pays better than the last one"

"Don't start again"

"You are two months late on your rent. Giving up a good career in the force for this nonsense!"

"You never wanted me to join the force in the first place!"

"That's because I want you to be safe, that's all. You are still not safe and now you have no prospects and no money."

"Thanks for improving my self esteem Mom!"

Charlie walked to the front door.

"I will see you on Saturday"

April Edwards watched as her son drove away. She had run her own dress shop in the town for twenty-five years. She gave it up when her husband died, not feeling that she needed her own money any more. She kept the shop in case she changed her mind and rented it out to a charity at a peppercorn rent. Charlie had the second floor room as his office. She worried about Charlie all the time, she thought he lacked direction in his life. She was trying to push him to extend himself. But the more she pushed the more he resisted. Perhaps she should take a different approach.

Charlie was steaming as he drove away from his mother's house, partly because she never gave encouragement and partly because she was right. Perhaps he should give himself a time limit and if it didn't work out he should try the police force again. The idea upset him but it was the only thing he felt qualified to do. He looked at the clock on the dashboard - three thirty. Time to go back to the office and check for any messages and then stroll round to the King's Head.

Charlie stood at the bar deciding whether to try the guest ale or go with his normal tipple when Peter walked into the bar.

"Perfect timing! I'll have my usual please."

Charlie ordered and they watched the landlord draw the beers, like watching an artist at work. They settled into a seat by the front window, which was open to allow a summer breeze to drift through the room.

"Well, what did you find out?"

Peter pulled a disc, in a clear plastic sleeve, out of his pocket and put it on the table.

"Quite a bit really, I could still be there now but for the deadline and the beer."

He took a drink and smacked his lips.

"Just the job"

"Never mind the beer, give me an outline."

"Killjoy! OK. As we established, the painting went missing for over two years, to be recovered by the Italian police."

"So it could have been copied"

"Yes the guy that stole it claimed he kept it in a trunk for all that time"

"And they didn't think it was copied at the time?"

"No evidence"

"So it is still a strong possibility"

"Oh yes. I found a piece by a reporter in 1931 stating that he had interviewed the guy behind the theft and that he forged four copies"

Charlie's jaw dropped open.

"Four?"

"Yes four"

They both picked up their beers at the same time and took a long thirsty drink.

"Are you going to tell me what this is all about?"

"No not yet. I haven't taken the case yet but if I do, I will need your help with the history."

"OK. When will you make up your mind?"

"I have another meeting in the morning, I will know then"

"Give me a call when you have decided"

Peter emptied his glass, looked at Charlie, looked at the glass, looked at Charlie, looked at the glass.

"OK, ok, same again"

"I thought you would never ask!"

CHAPTER NINETEEN

Charlie looked at the time in the bottom corner of the screen.

He had been in his office since eight o'clock and it was now ten. Wading through the information Peter had provided was fascinating but he felt like his brain had clogged up. Information overload! Time for breakfast. He switched the machine off and plucked his jacket from the hook on the back of the door. He was just about to pull the door to when the phone rang.

"Good morning Charlie"

It was Zoe.

"That was good timing. I was just on my way out the door"

"I am calling to see if you are going to take the case"

"Well yes but I need as much information as Lily can give me."

"As we said yesterday, we have the files my Grandfather prepared."

It struck Charlie strange that she should call James Barker her Grandfather, but on reflection he was, if only the common law variety.

"I can collect those and make a start today"

"I will be here all day"

She gave Charlie the address and he said he would call at about eleven o'clock.

The house stood on the top of the hill and was in a previous life a grand manor house. Having had time to grab a bacon sandwich and a coffee before leaving the town, Charlie now approached the house along a tree lined driveway. Converted into apartments Charlie imagined that Lily shared one with her granddaughter. He pulled to a halt on the gravel and got out of his car. The front door opened and Zoe stood in the doorway looking more casual than the day before. Designer jeans and a low cut t-shirt. The makeup was subdued and perfect.

"You found it all right?"

"Yes, I used to play with my friends down by the lake when I was at school."

"Used to bunk off school a lot, did you?"

"Boys will be boys!"

She stepped back from the doorway and gestured for him to enter the hallway.

"This is very grand."

"Well it was run down when we bought it, holes in the roof and all, but we are happy with the end result."

"So you own the whole building?"

"Yes, we converted it into four apartments. Lily has this one and mine is on the second floor. The others we rent out on long term leases. I wanted to share with Lily, take the whole ground floor but she said that she didn't want me fussing over her day and night and to know I was just upstairs was good enough. I think she was really thinking of me having my space."

Zoe led Charlie through the door into Lily's apartment.

"Lily is out this morning. She has a better social life than I do."

"That's a shame. I would have liked to ask her some more questions"

"Well I hope I can help and I can always relay the questions to her when she gets back. I have put some coffee on, should be ready any minute."

They entered the lounge, which had views down to the lake. The decoration was tasteful and understated. Charlie was continually being surprised by Lily and Zoe. On the table in the corner was a cardboard file box, Zoe pointed at it.

"That's all the information from Grandfather. Take a look and I'll see if the coffee is ready."

"Thanks"

Zoe left the room. He could hear the rattling of cups coming from what he presumed was the kitchen. The box looked new, he lifted the lid. It was full. He would need Peter's help to sort through this lot. Charlie looked at the top sheet of paper. A ship's manifest for the Mauretania 1910.

He was so engrossed that Zoe startled him when she asked if he took sugar.

"Yes please"

And seeing the two mugs on the tray

"Two spoons please"

Zoe sat down after putting Charlie's coffee on the table beside the chair opposite hers. Charlie saw this as a request to leave his treasure trove and come and sit down.

"So Charlie, what's the plan?"

"Well what I would like to do is take the file away, analyse what we have to work with, then come back to you with some idea about how we go forward. How does that sound?"

Charlie took a sip of his coffee, good stuff.

"That sounds ok to me, but Lily wanted a commitment that you would see it through."

"She can have that commitment once I have been through that box."

Charlie gestured at the box with his thumb.

"Ok. Twenty four hours, then I want an answer."

Charlie finished his coffee. Zoe leant forward while drinking hers, showing ample cleavage in the process.

"I will use an associate, an ex-police officer to help me look through the files."

"Fine. What's his name?"

"Why?"

"Lily will ask me and she probably knows him anyway"

"Peter Jenkins"

"Please put his time down as an expense"

"That I will. Well I better get on with it"

Charlie stood to leave, replaced the lid on the box file and was about to make for the door.

"Charlie, there's one other thing"

Charlie turned round to see Zoe standing by a very ordinary looking picture on the wall. She pulled the painting at its side and it hinged away from the wall and then turned on its axis. She then pushed it back against the wall to expose the rear of the frame. But instead of the rear of a very ordinary picture, this revealed the Mona Lisa.

Charlie's jaw dropped open. He had seen the one in the Louvre as a teenager and this one looked exactly as he remembered it.

"Oh my god!" was all he could say. As he was drawn towards the painting Zoe turned it back around.

"So we will talk tomorrow afternoon"

Charlie, still in a daze, stammered his agreement and was shown out. He stood in the driveway, box in hand and watched as Zoe was about to close the front door.

"Zoe, there is one question."

"Yes, what is it?"

"Has that painting been dated?"

"No never. Part of the request is that all the owners of the paintings must agree to testing or none will be tested. That's the way Grandfather wanted it."

Without another word Zoe shut the front door leaving Charlie with the box.

Charlie pulled the car to halt at the bottom of the drive and opened his phone.

"Pete, it's me. Are you free?"

"No"

"Oh!"

"I'm very expensive."

"No - I mean have you got free time this afternoon?"

"God, you are easy to wind up. Shall I see you at your office?"

"Yes — I will see you there."

Charlie closed his phone, spinning his wheels on the gravel drive as he pulled away and headed back into Lichfield.

CHAPTER TWENTY

Pete was waiting for him when he arrived. Charlie pushed the box at Pete so he could get his keys out of pocket.

"Not a lot of weight to it" Pete nodded at the box he was holding.

Charlie fumbled the door open and stood aside for Pete to go first.

"Age before beauty"

"Cheeky sod!"

They reached the top of the stairs that opened out into Charlie's office space. Windows to the front and rear let in plenty of light. Charlie had his desk facing the rear window. This gave him views across Minster pool to the cathedral.

Pete peered through the window.

"It is no wonder you never do any work, with a view like that to look at."

"Now who's being a cheeky sod?"

Pete had placed the box on a table by the front window. They both stood and looked at it.

Pete spoke.

"Well unless you are expecting the lid to jump off of its own volition, one of us should open it."

Charlie removed the lid and placed it on the floor. They both peered inside. Pete lifted out the content piece by piece.

A ship's manifest.

A menu from the captain's table.

Leather bound journal.

A file of newspaper clippings.

A letter.

Charlie removed the letter from the envelope and read it out loud.

"If you are reading this letter, you have agreed to help in my quest. I am of strong belief that the Mona Lisa in the Louvre is a copy. I hope that when you have read my Journal you will be like-minded.

Being infirm in my latter years, there has been many nuggets of information I have been unable to act upon, I hope you will have the stamina to see my quest through. I have never wanted to own the original painting or to embarrass the Louvre. But I have always felt that the owner of the original has a right to know.

There are such sophisticated ways of testing objects today that authentication will be easy.

I hope that you are now as intrigued as I have become over these many years and that you can fulfil the task ahead.

Yours Sincerely

James Barker Esq."

Charlie blew out his cheeks.

"Sounds crazy to me, but it is intriguing."

Pete picked up the journal and turned to the white board Charlie had installed on the one wall of his office. Picking up a marker pen off the ledge he opened the journal. He scanned the first page.

"The first entry goes back some twenty years."

"Well Zoe and Lily told me it was his obsession."

"It starts with him pondering on the possibility that the painting is real, and a subsequent visit he made to a Lady Sinclair, she being the great niece of the former owner of the painting and he being Earl Spencer Harcourt-Smythe."

"Hang on, that name rings a bell."

Charlie looked at the documents on the table in front of him

"Here it is. The ship's passenger list for the Mauretania, his name is on it."

Pete continued.

"He goes on about how disinterested Lady Sinclair was and how disdainful she was of her great uncle. Apparently he gambled away the family fortune and never did an honourable thing in his life. In short she didn't help at all apart from saying that the painting was used to pay a gambling debt."

"Is she still around?"

Pete put the journal down and switched on Charlie's computer.

While it powered up, he started to write on the white board, asking Charlie to confirm the date of the passenger list. He wrote next to it, COMMON DENOMINATOR, a question mark and circled it. He went back to computer and started a search.

"Well she's alive, in her eighties and lives in London."

"Looks like I will be on the train in the morning. Let's see if she has mellowed with age."

"So you are going to take the case?"

"With your help sifting through this lot and applying your computer know- how, yes. I will give Zoe a call later to let Lily know."

"And while you are in London I will carry on with the journal"

"Yes please."

They carried on and listed the names of all of the first class passengers on the board, some forty in total. With there being fifteen couples, the total came down to twenty-five names to work though, take out Eduardo and the Earl and they were down to twenty three names as possible art buyers.

Although they were aware that they were being led by Barker's journal and not by their own conclusions, it still seemed a logical place to start, and as neither of them were one to look a gift horse in the mouth, they decided to use the journal to build up a profile and timetable of events.

Pete looked at his watch.

"Time for the first down payment on my services."

Charlie looked at his watch and shrugged.

"OK. I could do with a bite to eat as well."

Pete smiled

"That's nice of you. It will save me cooking when I get home."

"I fell right into that one! Let's go."

CHAPTER TWENTY ONE

Charlie sat on the train to London Euston, contemplating the last forty-eight hours of his life. He had stumbled on to a case that was bigger than anything he had worked on before. Had he bitten off more than he could chew or would this be the catalyst that would take his business to new heights?

He had given Pete a key to his office and told him to carry on building a profile and date line of events. His conversation with Zoe had been to the point and business like. She did seem impressed that he would be going down to London the following morning, to follow up a lead. But she was trying to play him. She wanted him to be interested in her and he felt that was just so she could reject him. She was attractive, and far more sophisticated that the women he usually met, so was he just feeling his own inferiority and insecurity coming to the surface. Only time would tell.

The train arrived on time. He hated Euston, probably the least romantic of stations he had ever seen. He hurried outside to call Pete. His first task this morning was to find an address for Lady Sinclair.

The phone was ringing.

"Whitehall1212, Corner of the Yard speaking."

This was Pete being funny, the phone number being the old number for Scotland Yard and the name being a play on words attributed to Spike Milligan.

"Pete, it could have been anybody calling."

"That's why you have a phone with caller ID."

"Sorry I forgot that. Have you got the address?"

"Yes it is …

Charlie made a note of the address in Kensington.

"That's where I imagined she would be living."

"Yes sounds stereotypical."

"I will call you when I am out of the meeting, that's if I ever get in."

"Positive thinking, my boy, positive thinking."

Charlie closed his phone without giving a comeback, and made his way to the taxi rank.

The taxi dropped him off outside a nineteen-thirties' built apartment building. He hoped there wasn't a doorman. There was, but he was lucky because as he approached the door to the reception hall, he saw a uniform disappear into the lift with a parcel. This meant that he would have to use the stairs but the apartment he sought was only on the third floor. He arrived on the landing and took a minute to catch his breath and straighten his tie. It had been some time since he had worn one and he knew there would be a welt around his neck where the collar had rubbed.

He knocked and heard footsteps on what he imagined were polished wooden floors. The lock turned and was opened on a chain. Through the gap, he spied a grey haired woman in her sixties.

"Yes. Can I help you?"

"I would like to see Lady Sinclair Please."

"And you are?"

Charlie passed a card through the gap. At the same time there was a voice shouting from inside the apartment.

"Agnes, who is it?"

Agnes looked at Charlie.

"One moment please."

She turned away from the door

"It's a private detective, my Lady."

"How old is he?"

"What's that got to do with anything?"

"Just answer the question."

"Under thirty."

"Is he good looking?"

"Sort of."

"Oh Agnes, sometimes you are no help at all. You had better show him in and I can make up my own mind."

Agnes looked through the gap in the door and saw that Charlie had coloured up.

"Sorry about that. She is quiet harmless really."

With that, the door was pushed to and the chain was released. The door opened to reveal Agnes in a tweed suit, hair in a bun, sensible shoes, standing on a polished oak parquet floor. Agnes gestured for Charlie to enter. Charlie thanked her, waited while she relocked the door and followed her lead into the lounge. The room was crammed full of antiques, many out of place for the design of the apartment. In the centre of the room stood a very ornate chaise longue and upon it lay Lady Sinclair.

Charlie could only marvel at the make-up and hair. To say that she had been exuberant with the blusher was an understatement.

Her hair, which was pink, radiated from her head giving her a halo. A gold embroidered kimono set off the whole effect.

"Do sit down young man, would you like a drink?"

"Water would be fine. Thank you."

"Agnes, get the young man a glass of water and I will have my usual."

"Is it not a little early?"

"Nonsense, we have company."

Charlie could not see the reasoning behind that one.

"Are you married?"

"No, not as yet."

"Well you need a woman, young man. Oh yes every man needs a woman unless you lean in the other direction. You don't, do you?"

"No!"

"Good. It always seems such a waste to me."

Agnes returned with the drinks just in time to stop the conversation going further out of Charlie's control. Agnes passed across the water and Charlie noticed that they both had what appeared to be gin and tonics. Agnes noticed Charlie looking at her glass and offered an explanation.

"My Lady is opposed to drinking alone."

With that, Agnes's neck went red, indicting that it was only a half-truth.

Agnes passed Charlie's card to Lady Sinclair. She put on the half-moon glasses that had been hanging by a chain around her neck and inspected the card. This transformed her Ladyship's manner, all business and bluster.

"Well young man, what do you want?"

"I have been asked to enquire about a painting and I believe your family used to be custodians of said painting."

"We used to own most of the worthy works of art this country has ever seen. Which one have you in mind?"

"It was a copy of the Mona Lisa."

Agnes said "Oh Dear"

Charlie watched as Lady Sinclair went scarlet and shouted.

"Spencer's folly, that good for nothing playboy, squandered the family's fortune, built over five generations and frittered away in twenty years."

Charlie trying to defuse the situation before the old dear had a heart attack.

"Lady Sinclair, I didn't come here to upset you. It would be better if I left."

Charlie went to stand.

"Stay sat young man, if you open a can of worms you must at least take a good look. Now why do you think I live here?"

"Because it is very convenient?"

"No because that ruddy Spencer gambled away the family fortune and the last two generations have been trying to hang on to our country seat.

It's now been turned into ten luxury apartments and the stable block into mews cottages. What a waste! I have a few pieces of family furnishings around me but all else has been sold off."

"I am sorry to have brought this to the surface again and to cause you anguish."

Agnes chipped in.

"It is never very far from the surface Mr. Edwards."

"Charlie, please."

"OK. Charlie."

Agnes replied coyly.

Lady Sinclair cleared her throat making Agnes and Charlie turn towards her.

"Well Mr. Edwards, what in particular can I help you with?"

"Do you know how the painting was obtained and when?"

"I have no knowledge of any of the facts about the fake."

This was said with distain.

"Then I will be going, thank you for seeing me and your time."

Charlie again made to leave.

Lady Sinclair barked.

"Not so fast. Agnes, get the letter out of the top drawer of the bureau."

Agnes crossed the room and found the letter and handed it to Her Ladyship.

"This letter was found when we had a final clear out before we moved here. You can have it, if it will help in your quest, on one condition. Do you agree?"

Charlie by now just wanted to leave and would have said anything to escape this apartment.

"Yes I agree."

Lady Sinclair held out the envelope saying.

"You must return and tell us when you have found them all"

Charlie smiled. The old Lady knew what was going on all along.

Charlie took the letter and opened it. His jaw dropped open. So it was true, Eduardo de Valfierno was the master con artist all along.

"Makes interesting reading, does it not?"

"It certainly does."

Charlie put the letter in his pocket.

"Thank you for that. It verifies our thoughts and helps point us in the right direction."

"Charlie, you are most welcome."

That was the first time she had addressed him as Charlie.

"I will be in touch when I have completed my investigation."

"Agnes, give Charlie one of my cards."

Agnes produced a card from the pocket of her tweed suit and passed it to Charlie.

"Phone so we can tell the doorman of your impending arrival for your next visit."

"Certainly and thank you."

Lady Sinclair held out her hand to bid Charlie farewell. As he took her hand out of politeness, she pulled him towards her with strength that surprised Charlie and ended with him getting a kiss on the cheek. Agnes coloured up and then admonished Charlie for letting it happen. Lady Sinclair laughed like a banshee.

Agnes showed Charlie to the door.

"She will be hell to live with for the rest of the day."

Charlie turned in the doorway and pecked Agnes on the cheek.

"I hope that makes it a little easier."

Agnes coloured up and shooed him out the door.

Charlie stood there wondering if he had dreamt the last hour. As he walked away he could hear the both of them cackling.

He decided to walk through Kensington Gardens to clear his head. He wanted to re-read the letter so stopped at a park bench, took a couple of deep breaths and took the envelope from his pocket. It was so tantalizing. It confirmed the existence and involvement of the forgers but didn't name the purchasers. He phoned Peter.

"Battersea Dogs Home."

Charlie decided to ignore the opening.

"Pete, I have a letter sent by Eduardo de Valfierno."

"So we aren't on a wild goose chase."

"That's right. It confirms that old Barker wasn't barking after all."

"Charlie, it's better if you leave the jokes to me in the future. Well, read it to me."

Charlie cleared his throat and quoted from the letter.

"I am writing with reference to your purchase of a certain painting two years ago.

Four persons purchased the painting, which was produced from the original by probably the most talented living artist of the day. The artist has recently informed me that the original is <u>not</u> the painting that has been returned to the Louvre. This means you have a one in four chance that your painting is the genuine article. You will hear that the Louvre have ways of knowing that theirs is the original, but it is not true. Please be assured that this letter is sent in good faith and while you were misled in your original purchase, the artist and myself hoped that this would offer some solace.

Yours with honourable intentions."

"That takes this on to another level of intrigue. When will you be back?"

"I will catch the next train, should get me there mid afternoon. See you then."

"OK. See you later."

Charlie could hear in Pete's voice that he was already preoccupied with the case. He folded the letter carefully and put it back in his pocket and made for the nearest taxi rank.

CHAPTER TWENTY TWO

Charlie left the train, retrieved his car from the car park and made his way back into town. He had sat on the train pondering what direction the case would take them. They knew as fact that originally there were four paintings produced. One of which Lily had in her apartment. That left three to locate. The Mauretania was their main lead. They knew the Earl was on board and so was Eduardo De Valfierno. This left the rest of the first class passengers to investigate.

He went up the stairs to his office two at a time.

Pete was that absorbed by what was on the computer screen in front of him that he didn't hear him coming.

"I wasn't expecting you till about four o'clock."

As he said this, Pete looked at the time in the bottom corner of the screen.

"No wonder my stomach is rumbling. It's nearly four now."

"Would you like me to go out and get you a sandwich?"

"That would be great, and a coffee."

"How is it going?"

"I will go through what I've got when you come back, but you can leave me the letter before you go."

Charlie passed across the letter and went down the stairs mumbling something about being the dogsbody. As he got to the front door Pete shouted down the stairs.

"And bring some donuts back as well."

Charlie shut the front door unable to think of a riposte, turned nearly colliding with Lily on her mobility scooter.

"For a private eye, you are not much good at looking where you are going, are you?"

"Sorry about that. I was going to phone Zoe with an update later."

"Oh were you Charlie?"

Charlie looked round to see Zoe looking casual but stylish. Shirt unbuttoned to reveal ample cleavage as usual.

"Well, how about you and your associate, come up for a spot of supper about eight this evening and you can fill us in on what you have been up to."

Lily chimed in.

"That sounds like a great idea."

Charlie stammered slightly

"Yes if Peter's free, I'm sure it would be fine."

They parted and Charlie had made five steps when Lily shouted after him.

"Neither of you are vegan, are you?"

Lily made it sound like an obscure religion.

"No Lily, anything will be fine for us."

Charlie walked away noting the delight Zoe enjoyed in Charlie's embarrassment.

They sat eating their sandwiches and drinking their coffee. Charlie knew Pete would be only too happy to accept the invitation, partly through curiosity, having never met them and mainly because he wouldn't have to cook for himself. Pete helped himself to a donut and proceeded to get jam on his chin, which he flicked into his mouth with his little finger.

"So we start with forty first class passengers' names, take out Eduardo and the Earl, leaves us thirty eight. There were fifteen couples, which reduces the number of names to twenty-three.

Charlie struggled to follow the logic then caught up.

"Twenty-three. That's still a long list to track down and contact."

"Yes. We will be contacting people out of the blue. If their families don't have the painting, they will think we are nuts. And if they do have one, why would they admit it to us?"

Pete stood up, licking the sugar off his fingers and walked over to the white board.

"If we use a process of elimination and try and locate the families that are nearest to us, it will save time. I will work through all the UK citizens first and see what that brings us. As soon as I have a contact, you can follow it up."

"Seems like a plan to me. How long will it take?"

Peter looked at the board.

"Well fourteen of the names look English and I know where to look to trace them. But for the others, I will be starting from scratch. They look French, German and Dutch."

"That's your starting point tomorrow. I will assist with copious cups of coffee."

Peter doing a poor impersonation of Homer Simpson

"And donuts!"

"OK and donuts."

CHAPTER TWENTY THREE

They turned off the road onto the gravel driveway, which led up to the house.

Charlie had picked Pete up from his home. They had briefly discussed what to wear on parting in the afternoon and decided on smart casual. The only problem was in their interpretation of the phrase. Pete was in a pair of fawn trousers, button down shirt and blazer. Charlie had on his best pair of jeans, with creases and a polo shirt with a little crocodile motif on the breast. Pete's shoes, polished to within an inch of their lives, Charlie's having never seen polish in their lives. Charlie shook his head on seeing Pete, talk about being from a different world.

Charlie knew Pete would know how to behave but had to give him a reminder.

"Now Pete, remember they are the client and we work for them."

"As your former senior officer, I think I know how to conduct myself."

"Sorry Pete. These sorts of things make me nervous."

"You are so easily wound up."

"Sod!"

"I hope you won't be using language like that in front of the ladies."

Pete rebuked.

Charlie just shook his head.

As they pulled up to the entrance the light above the door came on, Charlie couldn't tell if by sensor or manually. As he locked the car, the door opened to reveal Zoe, back lit from the hall light.

"Good evening gentlemen."

Charlie made the introductions as they walked in to the hallway. The door to Lily's apartment was ajar and Zoe led the way in to the lounge

Zoe asked what they would like to drink and she excused herself to get them and see how Lily was doing in the kitchen.

"Nice place." Pete whispered to Charlie.

"Yes they own the whole building."

"Do they now? Very nice."

Charlie wondered if Pete knew something that he didn't. Zoe returned with their drinks followed by Lily walking with a stick. This was the first time he had seen her standing up. She was quiet tall even at her age. Charlie could see that she would have been a very striking woman in her prime.

"Hello Lily, you are looking well."

Pete kissed Lily on both cheeks while Charlie watched on with a raised eyebrow.

Lily saw Charlie's expression.

"We go back a long way. Haven't you told him Peter?"

"Our personal life is none of his business."

Lily laughed out loud.

"Peter behave yourself! You will be giving him and Zoe the wrong idea."

Charlie looked at Zoe who shrugged her shoulders.

"Charlie, I've learnt not to ask, I sleep better that way."

Lily laughed again.

"Listen to mother over there."

They sat down and Lily explained.

"When Peter was in charge of the local police, we used to liaise on matters concerning the prostitutes in the town. I wasn't active but had become a mother figure to a lot of the girls so if he had a problem with one of them he would call on me, and if one of the girls had a problem with a customer, I would call on him. It seemed to work pretty well, all in all."

Pete smiled.

"Lily kept many a girl on the straight and narrow, which may sound daft but I always viewed prostitution as a profession and as long as they were discreet I would turn a blind eye. The problems come when drugs and pimps get involved."

"Yes then he would call on Aunty Lily to help with some counselling and for the most part we did some good."

Pete Laughed

"Many a night I would call Lily in to the police station to speak to some snivelling wretch of a girl who was too young and too frightened to speak to the police. Lily was invaluable to me in those situations. She could empathise with the girls, and understood the law. She was a very shrewd judge of character."

Lily actually blushed.

"There has been a lot of water under the bridge since then. Now we are both in a new chapter of our lives, new adventures, which includes our supper. I will go and see how it's coming along."

Lily steadied herself to her feet and made her way into the kitchen. They sat in silence for a few moments, sipping their drinks. Then Zoe excused herself to help her grandmother. As soon as she had left the room Charlie turned on Pete.

"Why the hell didn't you tell me you knew Lily?"

"Well I was going to, until you started lecturing me about how to behave."

"I apologised for that."

"It was too late by then, we were here."

"You enjoyed the surprise though, didn't you?"

Pete chuckled

"Oh yes. You face was a study to behold."

With that Zoe put her head around the door and announced that it was time to move into the dinning room.

The meal went without a hitch. A home-made celery soup to start followed by Moroccan lamb and finished off with a homemade bread and butter pudding. A menu designed for the guests, Charlie decided as he put down his napkin. They went through to the lounge for coffee and Zoe poured a brandy for three and a Bailey's for Lily. As they settled into their comfortable chairs, Zoe took a sip of her drink and looked across at Charlie.

"So what news have you for us?"

Charlie removed a copy of Eduardo's letter from his pocket and handed it to Zoe. She read it and smiled.

"Well, well, well. Where did you get this?"

Lily said.

"What is it? Read it to me."

Zoe read it out loud which produced a whistle from Lily.

"The old darling was right about it all along."

As she said this she gestured with her thumb towards the painting on the wall. Pete looked bemused, as he was the only one who didn't know what was hidden there.

Charlie nodded.

"I managed to speak with the Earl's descendant this morning and she passed the letter on. As you are the rightful owner of the painting she felt that the letter should be kept by you."

Zoe smiled,

"So Grandfather was right all along?"

"Yes and we feel he may have been on the right lines with his passenger list for the Mauretania. That will be our starting point tomorrow."

They finished their coffee, lost in their own thoughts. Finally Pete stretched and yawned. So Charlie said.

"That's a sign that we should be going."

"Sorry I yawned, no reflection on the company, but there is one thing before we go, could I see the painting?"

Lily laughed.

"Oh Peter, I was forgetting you haven't seen it!"

Lily struggled to her feet and walked to the nondescript painting on the wall, hinged it away from the wall and turned it.

Pete and Charlie both rose in unison and walk to the picture.

"Oh My God", was all that Pete could say.

CHAPTER TWENTY FOUR

Over the next two days they worked on the twenty-three names, starting with the English sounding names. They squared off the white board so that every name had its own box, adding information to the box, as it was determined. With only a name as a lead, the process was slow. They managed to eliminate four couples, three had been on honeymoon to New York, they discussed them as potential buyers and decided that even if they had the money they would probably not be interested in the Mona Lisa. Peter wrote 'Unlikely' across there boxes. The husband of the fourth couple had travelled back from New York in the hospital ward on board with heart problems. Charlie had made ten phone calls in all and only the four had been fruitful. He was getting impatient.

"Surely there has got to be something else I can be doing."

Pete looked up from his laptop and sighed.

"Apart from the coffee, you are starting to be a nuisance."

Pete looked at the board

"How is your German?"

"School boy stuff. I can order a beer, ask for directions, that sort of thing."

"Well have a go at the Teidermar, they are the only German sounding name on the list. At least you can eliminate them from our list."

Charlie blew out his cheeks and sat in front of the screen. Not ever having done a search before, he just went into his browser and typed in the name.

"I have fifty hits and they are mostly looking Austrian."

"Good, that will give you something to do. Go into each one and see what they are. Remember we are looking for old money, pre world war one."

"This will take forever!"

"Patience was never your strong suit, was it?"

Peter looked across at Charlie. He hadn't interrupted him for an hour and the silence was deafening.

"OK. How are you doing?"

"Well, I don't know but there is one that might be worth a phone call. It's a vineyard owner in Austria."

"Well, they won't have had it so good over the last few years after the antifreeze scandal."

"It says here that they are one of the largest producers of red wine in Austria and that over seventy percent of the wine is consumed in Austria."

"Any history?"

"Yes, been in the same family for over one hundred years."

"It's worth a call then."

"Why don't you go and get us a sandwich while I make the call?"

"So you don't want an audience then?"

"No. Especially you!"

"What do you think I will do?"

"I hate to think, but you would think of something."

"OK. What do you want?"

Charlie gave his order and Peter left to purchase lunch.

Charlie picked up the phone and dialled the number on the pad.

A voice answered the phone in English with a strong Austro-German accent.

"Teidermar Vineyards"

"Could I speak to Herr Teidermar please?"

"That is not possible as he is out in the vineyard. Can I be of help?"

"It is a personal matter with regarding a painting which may have been purchased by his family, one hundred years ago. Can I leave my number and ask that he contact me?"

"One moment please I will try and contact him on his walkie-talkie. He will not take his phone with him when he tends to the grapes."

The phone went dead for a few minutes.

"Hello"

"Yes?"

"Herr Teidermar will be available for the next three days. If you wish to speak of this matter, you must see him in person. Will you come?"

Charlie stammered.

"Yes."

"I will inform Herr Teidermar. Goodbye."

The phone went dead and Charlie sat there with the phone in his hand. He was pulled out of his stupor by Peter climbing the stairs singing 'coughs and sneezes spread diseases' to the tune of Deutschland Deutschland uber alles.

Peter took one look at Charlie and said.

"Whatever is wrong?"

"I've got to go to Austria."

"You mean you have located one of the paintings?"

"Yes I think so."

"Well either you have or you haven't."

"Well I didn't speak to the guy himself, but his right hand man said that he would only speak about it in person and he would be available for the next three days."

"Well it sounds like you are going to Austria. You jammy git! I've been slogging away for the best part of two day with the only results for my efforts being negative ones and in five minutes you find a bloody painting."

"Beginner's luck!"

"Dumb luck more like! Better find out where it is and book a flight."

"Lunch first."

They ate lunch in silence, both lost in their own thoughts. Peter cleared the debris of lunch from his desk and stretched.

"If you take a copy of the letter with you, it will prove to him that you are representing another owner of the painting. Try and see if there was a journal kept by his ancestors. It may hold some clues."

Charlie nodded in agreement.

"This case is getting odder by the day. I wonder where it will lead us next."

"Well you to Austria and me stuck in front of the computer."

"I'd better have a look at the nearest airport and book a flight."

They fell into silence as they both concentrated on the screens in front of them.

"Bratislava"

"I beg your foul-mouthed pardon!"

"That's the nearest airport, flying from Birmingham tomorrow morning."

"Want a lift to the airport."

"I have to be there for seven am."

"So you will be taking your own car then?"

Charlie gave Peter an old-fashioned look.

"I know who my friends are then!"

"Ok, I will pick you up at six fifteen."

"Thanks"

CHAPTER TWENTY FIVE

Charlie was driving south out of Vienna. He had phoned Zoe the previous night to tell her about the trip, then packed an overnight bag and had an early night.

The flight had gone without a hitch. He had picked up a hire car from the airport, driven the twenty miles across the border from Bratislava to Vienna and was now driving through rolling countryside with mountains as a back drop on a beautiful day. The most trying part of the day so far had been Peter being so chirpy at six fifteen in the morning. He had had no idea that Peter was such a morning person, though he suspected that he was overplaying it just to be irritating.

He came over the brow of a hill and his sat-nav told him to turn right off the main road. He passed through a town with a railway station and took a left on to a smaller lane, rounded a bend and the house was in front of him. Imposing with the sun shining of the grey tiled roof. He entered through the gateway in a high stonewall and entered a stone flagged courtyard. The only other vehicle parked there was golf cart. As he opened the car door, a man came out of the main entrance and strode over to him.

"You would be Charlie, yes? I am Klaus. We spoke on the phone."

Charlie became all British.

"Very nice to meet you Klaus."

Charlie took his bag from the car.

"I will take that and put it in your room, you will stay the night, yes?"

"That's very nice of you."

Charlie wondered why he was coming over all 'Jeeves and Wooster', and decided that it was the Germanic accent that was doing it to him.

"Would you like to toilet or are you ready to meet Herr Teidermar?"

"I can wait till later thank you."

"Good then we go."

Klaus pointed to the golf cart and walked across and put Charlie's overnight bag in the box that was built on the back. Charlie hesitated to join Klaus then jumped in beside him. They left the courtyard by another gateway and proceeded between what appeared to be farm buildings.

"That is the wine press."

Klaus pointed to a large stone built barn.

"You will see it all later"

To Charlie it sounded like an order rather than an invitation.

They left the buildings behind and entered field upon field of grape vines.

Charlie was frantically trying to remember his German from school but knew that his host's English would be far better than his German. They bounced along the rutted tracks between the vines and the speck of a human being in the distance became larger. Even at a distance the person looked younger than he had expected and as they approached he realised that Herr Teidermar was perhaps in his late twenties or early thirties.

They pulled to a halt at the end of a row of vines, at which point the stooping person rose and walked towards the golf cart.

Charlie got out, Klaus remained behind the wheel. Herr Teidermar spoke a sentence in his native tongue to Klaus. Klaus nodded and drove away.

"You must be Charles. Jolly nice to meet you. Did you have a good trip?"

The strong Oxbridge accent took Charlie by surprise.

"Very good thank you and please call me Charlie."

Herr Teidermar held out his hand.

"And you must call me Hans. Sorry to drag you out into the fields but actually tending the vine is a self-imposed penance. Some people think I'm mad, but it helps me keep it real."

Hans used the first two fingers of both hands to form quotation marks either side of his head.

"It must be good to be hands-on, to feel that you are involved in creating the wine."

"My grandfather and my father showed me how and I hope to show a son of mine one day. If you will allow me to finish this row I will call it a day."

Charlie walked along as Hans finished the row watching the care he gave to his task. When they reached the end they walked up to the top of the field where a quad-bike was parked. Hans put his tools in the box at the rear and mounted the bike.

"Hop on and hold on tight."

Charlie had no choice but to do as instructed.

CHAPTER TWENTY SIX

Charlie lay on the bed in his room and stared at the ceiling, reflecting on his day and his newfound friend. Hans was passionate about his heritage, his vineyards, and the family business.

"We produce the best wine in Austria." He boasted but Charlie knew that he meant it with real sincerity. But underlying all the bravado, there was a sorrow about Hans to which Charlie couldn't put his finger on.

He had whisked Charlie around the estate on the quad-bike showing him the wine-making process up to the finished article they would sample this evening. The house was not as big as it appeared from a distance. The design gave the illusion of grandeur but was of the size of a manor house rather than a stately home. The decoration was traditional in the main but his room had been modernised with white walls and Ikea style furnishings and a newly appointed adjoining bathroom. Charlie had an hour before meeting with Hans. They had not talked about paintings or his family history but Hans just said in passing that he had something of interest to show him this evening.

Charlie changed into a clean pair of chinos and an open neck shirt and made his way downstairs. As he entered the hallway Klaus appeared and gestured towards a door that was ajar. Charlie walked through the door and Klaus followed.

"Herr Teidermar will be here in a moment. I must offer you a drink."

Charlie could not resist it.

"You must."

Klaus's colour rose.

"I'm sorry for my bad English."

"I am a guest and I speak no German, so it is I who should apologise."

Klaus gave a little nod of his head.

"May I offer you a drink?"

"Thank you. That would be very agreeable. Do you have a dry sherry?"

"I will return."

With that Klaus left the room. Charlie looked around. He stood in a small baronial hall, with vaulted ceiling and a large stone fireplace. Four winged armchairs faced the fire in a semi circle. Charlie was drawn to a selection of framed photographs on an elegant side table by the far wall.

The oldest photos appeared to be Victorian showing a moustachioed gentleman standing next to the wine press Hans had shown him earlier. There was an array of family groups spanning the last hundred years but in the centre at the front was a modern image of Hans with a very attractive girl standing in one of the vineyards. Charlie picked it up and could see that their closeness was genuine and not just for the camera.

Klaus appeared with his sherry as Charlie replaced the photograph.

"Is the lady joining us this evening?"

"Marie is dead."

"I am sorry."

"Two years ago, very sudden, a shock."

The door opened and Klaus turned towards it as if he had been caught out. He obviously thought he had talked out of turn. Hans walked in and asked what Charlie was drinking, then asked Klaus to bring him the same.

"First, I thought we would discuss business then we can enjoy our meal without wondering if we are playing the same game."

Charlie nodded his agreement.

"Firstly, Charlie please tell me who you are and what you have to do with all this?"

"Well as I said on the phone I am a private detective, an ex-police officer. I have a client who has inherited a painting with a puzzle attached. My job is to locate three identical paintings and if, and only if all parties are agreeable then arrange for the paintings to be tested for authenticity."

Charlie passed across a business card. Hans looked at it and put it on a side table.

"This tells me who you are but I need proof that your client is an owner."

Charlie reached into the back pocket of his chinos and produced a folded A4 sheet of paper. He passed it to Hans. Hans got to his feet and went to the side table and opened a drawer. Turning back towards Charlie, Hans had what looked like a photo album. He turned two pages and passed it to Charlie. There in front of him was the self same letter. Charlie stared at the page.

"Do you still have the painting?"

Hans smiled and nodded towards an alcove with a velvet curtain at the far end of the room. Charlie had noted the recess earlier but thought it was a doorway. Hans made no move to show Charlie the painting.

"It is a family treasure. We were told stories about it as children but it wasn't until I was old enough to read my great-great grand mother's journal that I found out the real truth."

"You have a journal?"

"Oh yes. It is not that exciting really, just about her voyage to America."

"Does she talk about her travelling companions?"

"Yes and a boring lot they appeared to be for the most."

Charlie started to fidget in his seat, leaning forward in his seat.

"We are having trouble tracking down the other owners and believe that they may have been on the same ship as your descendant."

"Well we can take a look at the journal and see if there are any clues you can use."

Just as Charlie was about to ask to see the journal the door opened and Klaus said that dinner was ready.

Hans led the way out of the room and up the main stairs. On the landing they paused at an iron bound door.

"I hope you don't mind but I thought we would dine alfresco."

Hans opened the door to reveal a spiral stone staircase. They climbed forty steps, Charlie counted them, and came to a small landing with another iron bound door. Hans opened it and stepped out. Charlie followed and caught his breath. They stood on the roof with views overlooking the whole valley, vineyards as far as the eye could see.

"This is magnificent."

"My parents never used the space up here but I have always loved it. In my youth, I would bring many a young lady up here."

There was a momentary twinkle in his eye, and then it was gone as if he had thought that he should not have happy memories. They took their seats under an awning. The appetizer was already in place, smoked salmon. Hans poured them both a glass of ice-cold white wine.

"This is a dry white. I hope you enjoy its depth of flavour."

Charlie sipped the white wine, which was a perfect accompaniment to the salmon and hoped that Hans wouldn't get too intense about the wine tasting. Charlie liked a bottle of wine with the best of them, but couldn't distinguish between one grape and another.

The meal progressed with a different wine for each course, all of which Charlie thought were great. They didn't mention the painting or the journal though Charlie was itching to see it. Charlie was intrigued by the façade that Hans put forward. Keen to talk about his family and the business but stopping short of talking about himself. Finally after coffee, as they were stood next to each other taking in the view, Charlie could not resist asking the question.

"My mother thinks I should be settled, with a wife and family at my age. Have you ever been temped to marry?"

"Charlie, it's something I find very hard to talk about. I was engaged to Marie, my childhood sweetheart."

Hans fell silent. Charlie waited for Hans to speak, knowing he would, given time.

"She died two years ago of a brain haemorrhage. Quite suddenly. She died in my arms."

Charlie could not help himself and put his arm around Hans's shoulder, feeling a silent sob from Hans.

"In the police force we were trained to console people at times like this but I always felt that words were so inadequate. Losing an older person from your life is terrible but to lose someone so young must be devastating. I can't offer you any words that haven't already been said by your family and friends but perhaps a break from here would help."

"I fear that if I leave I won't want to return. Too many memories you see."

Hans turned to face Charlie.

"I am sorry for behaving like this."

"You have nothing to apologise for, I asked you the question."

"Come we will go and get a proper drink."

Hans led the way down the stairs and back into the main hall. The fire was aglow and Charlie didn't realise that it had become so cold on the roof terrace, until the heat of the fire hit them as they entered. Hans went to a cabinet on the one wall.

"What is your poison?"

"Bourbon, straight please."

"No problem."

Hans passed Charlie his drink and then went to the side table and brought back the framed photo of him and Marie.

"There she is."

He passed the photo to Charlie.

"She was very pretty"

"Yes and a wicked sense of humour."

Hans paused and smiled

"This is strange. You are the first person I have talked to about Marie who did not know her."

Charlie realised that he was privileged and in a position to help Hans move his life forward. All he had to do was listen. For the next hour Charlie listened intently only nodding and prompting Hans to talk if he fell silent. Hans spoke about his life with Marie and their plans for the future. Hans smiled as he talked about her, then stopped in mid-sentence and looked at Charlie.

"Charlie, thank you for letting me ramble on. I think it has helped."

"Good."

"I was forgetting the journal."

He rose and went to the side table and pulled a small leather bound book out of the drawer together with a note pad and pen.

"You may need this to make notes."

Hans passed the note pad to Charlie.

"Now what are you interested in?"

"Well, any reference to the other passengers on board the Mauretania."

"I will translate as we go, providing I can read her writing."

Charlie waited patiently as Hans scanned the pages. About twenty pages in, his face brightened.

"This could be what you are looking for. My Great Greats were invited to the Captain's table."

"If she made a note of the other people around the table that would be really interesting."

Charlie doodled on the paper while he waited for Hans to find something of interest. He was feeling the benefits of the wine and bourbon and hoped he wasn't slurring his words for he saw no sign that Hans was anything but sober.

"Here we are."

Hans said loudly, looking up from the journal causing Charlie to jump.

"She goes on about the menu before she talks about the people around the table. So we can see where her priorities used to lie. Right around the table sat Eduardo De Valfierno, art dealer. Earl Harcourt-Smythe. George and Edith Adams, American bankers from New York. Chuck and Avril Parker, he, an oil baron."

"Well we know that two of the party bought a painting from Eduardo, so we had better check the others out. Thanks Hans, this is really helpful."

"I am happy to help."

Hans got up and refilled their glasses. Charlie knew he had had enough but it would have been impolite not to accept the ample measure of the warming liquid.

"Cheers. To the future."

Hans smiled at Charlie.

"To the future."

CHAPTER TWENTY SEVEN

Peter looked at the clock. Three fifteen in the morning.

He picked up his mobile phone that was vibrating across his bedside table. The screen said 'Charlie'. Peter fell back on to his pillow and pressed the receive button.

"Peter, it's Charlie."

"Yes I know and it's also three fifteen in the morning."

Charlie started to giggle.

"You are up early then."

"Charlie, that isn't my idea. Are you drunk?"

Charlie sounding sheepish "I might be."

"So, what do you want?"

"I've had a very nice time."

"Good for you. Now what do you want?"

Charlie started to giggle again.

"Why are you so grumpy? It's not as if you had been woken up in the middle of the night."

"Charlie I am going to switch off my phone now."

"No, no, paper and pen, paper and pen."

Peter opened the drawer and pulled out a pad and pen.

"What?"

"Hans's great great great great great grand mother, that may have been too many greats."

Charlie started to giggle again.

"Charlie I'm warning you!"

"Sorry. Anyway she kept a journal, which included her invitation to the Captain's table on the Maury, Mauryt, Mauryt, that boat."

Charlie giggled again. Peter bit his tongue.

"Her fellow diners that night included the Earl, Eduardo and the following guests, George and Edith Adams, bankers from New York and Chuck and Avril Parker, oil people from Texas."

"That's why I was having trouble finding them in England!"

"Anyway I can't be talking to you all night, it's past my bed time."

Peter could here Charlie giggling again as his phone went dead.

This was now a problem for Peter. He would be awake all night, itching to get on with finding these people while he knew Charlie was probably asleep as soon as he switched off his phone. It was no good. He would have to get up. He made a mental note to pay Charlie back in spades for waking him. The idea made him smile.

Charlie couldn't understand who was beating on the inside of his cranium. He came to, realising it was a knock on his bedroom door. His tongue felt like it was wearing a woollen mitten.

"Come in"

The door opened and Klaus entered with a tray of coffee.

"Hans hopes you are feeling well and wishes you a good trip. He has instructed me to offer you breakfast if you require and that you can stay as long as you like."

Charlie didn't believe that Klaus held the same good wishes for him to stay but in his state appreciated his candour.

"Hans has gone to attend to the vines. He said that it would be his penance for last night."

"Thank you Klaus but breakfast may be a mistake for me this morning and as I have a plane to catch I will leave as soon as I am dressed."

Klaus smiled as he turned to the door

"You will not take long then."

It was then that Charlie realised that he was still fully clothed from the previous night. As Klaus closed the door behind him, Charlie thanked him for the coffee and could hear him laughing as he walked away. He flopped back on to his pillow and stared at the ceiling. What a strange twenty-four hours. He then remembered that he had phoned Peter the night before and given him the other names. He can't have been in that bad a shape then. He sat up much too quickly and waited for things to stop revolving. He was wrecked. He looked at his watch. He had four hours before his flight but with the drive and check –in, he would need all of it. Getting slowly to his feet, he stripped to the waist, washed, cleaned his teeth, scrubbed his tongue, put on a fresh shirt and stuffed everything into his overnight bag. As he arrived in the hallway, Klaus appeared with a small foil parcel and handed it to him.

"You must have something in your stomach. It is burned bread." Charlie took a minute to focus.

"Ah yes, toast. Thank you Klaus, that is very nice of you."

They moved to the doorway, which Klaus opened. He held out his hand. Charlie shook it.

"Thanks again Klaus you have been most accommodating."

Charlie feeling he had lapsed into a P.G.Woodhouse caricature again.

"No I must thank you. You helped Herr Teidermar with your company, thank you."

Charlie said he would be in touch and turned to his car. By the time he had dropped into the front seat, the door had closed.

The journey back to the airport was uneventful, with the hire car returned and having checked-in Charlie had time to kill before his flight. The trip back to the airport had perked him up. He pulled out the notes he had made the previous night and decided to phone Peter.

"Hi, it's Charlie."

"I know it is you. What time is it?"

"Noon. Why?"

"Because some prat keeps waking me up."

"But it's the middle of the day."

"Not if some prat woke you up at three fifteen in the morning."

"That prat must have been me."

"That's why you are a detective."

"Sorry Peter."

"I'm awake now anyway, so what's news?"

"I've got a hangover and Hans is a really nice guy. Other than that only what I told you last night. How about you?"

"I will tell you when you get back but get used to the idea that you are going to America."

"What?"

"And I think you will need help when you get there."

"What?"

"What time will you be back?"

"I should be back in Lichfield about four."

"Good. I'll meet you in the Acorn."

"I don't think I will be drinking today."

"Good, all the more for me."

With that Charlie's phone went dead.

CHAPTER TWENTY EIGHT

Peter sat in a booth in the Acorn. He had a pint or what was left of a pint in front of him. He was doodling on his note pad and feeling jet lagged. His lack of sleep was catching up with him. A voice from behind him said.

"You look as bad as I feel."

Peter looked up to see Charlie standing there.

"I could say the same for you."

"What's your poison?"

"The usual."

"I'll be back in a bit."

Charlie went to the bar and Peter turned the page in his notebook back to the jotting he had made earlier in the day. Charlie put two pints on the table and sat down opposite with a sigh. Peter looked at the two pints.

"Are they both for me or have you changed your mind about drinking?"

Charlie picked up the pint nearest to him and took a long draft, put the glass down and looked at Peter.

"Well that answers my question."

Charlie smiled.

"So what have you found out?"

Peter looked down at his notebook.

"Adams, the New York banker's family is still in new York."

"Are they still in banking?"

"No. George lost everything in the crash and disappeared, leaving his wife and daughter to fend for themselves. But his great grandson is still listed."

"Well at least we have a starting point. What about the Parkers?"

"Still in oil, they sold out to Shell in the forties but retained stock and positions within the company. Their great-grandson is still working in the company."

"Another starting point!"

Peter finished his first pint and took a sip of the new one leaving a foam moustache on his upper lip. This amused Charlie who wanted to see how long it would last. Peter drew his tongue across his upper lip removing the foam. Life was full of little disappointments.

"Charlie, you are going to need help with this and it will come at a cost so you had better speak to Zoe."

"Yes, I was going to call Zoe with an update anyway, so I can tell them how we want to proceed."

"Well, how was Austria?"

Charlie sighed and started relating his trip. Peter nodded and smiled in the right places but didn't interrupt. Police training had stayed with him. Don't stop people speaking when they are in full flow, you never know what you may learn. So he saved his questions till Charlie stopped to take a drink.

"So you didn't bring any of his wine back with you then?"

"All you ever think about is food and drink."

Peter feigned a hurt look.

"I have my moments when I think of other things, but that's my business. Anyway go on with the story."

Charlie finished the tale and Peter blew out his cheeks.

"Sounds a bit strange, your friend Hans."

"He's been through a bad patch, needs time away from his wine, a change of scenery and routine and he will be a lot better."

Peter offered to get a round in but Charlie declined, much as it upset him to refuse a drink from Peter.

"No thanks. I had better go and speak to Zoe before it gets too late."

"Suit yourself. I'm off for my supper then and I will see you in the morning at the office."

They walked through the pub and out onto the pavement, Peter noting the bemused looks Charlie was getting from the other drinkers. As they were going in different directions, Charlie said "See you in the morning."

"Charlie?"

"Yes?"

"I should wipe that foam of your top lip before you see Zoe. We don't want you looking like a rabid dog, not good for business."

And with that Peter turned on his heels and disappeared down the street. Charlie wiped his mouth with his sleeve, removing the foam and realising that he needed a shave. Shaking his head at the disappearing figure of Peter, he made for home. Time for a quick shave and brush up and then he would call Zoe and see if he could pop round.

He felt tired as he pulled up to the door and realised that he hadn't eaten since the airport sandwich. He would bring Zoe up to speed and then make a swift exit. The prospect of his own bed and a full night's sleep brought a smile to his face. The front door was ajar, so he pushed it open and entered the hallway. Zoe looked down from the top of the stairs.

"Come on up. I'm just opening a bottle of wine."

Charlie looked up to see Zoe dressed in a skirt and her customary low cut top.

"Well come on, I won't bite."

As she turned to re-enter her apartment, her skirt twirled exposing a peach of a backside and a thong. Charlie approached the first step feeling like Benjamin to Zoe's Mrs Robinson. With every step of the stairs he repeated the mantra 'do not get involved with the clients'. He arrived at the front door, as Zoe appeared from the kitchen with two glasses of wine.

Who was he kidding?

CHAPTER TWENTY NINE

Charlie came awake with a realisation that there was somebody in his bedroom. He could hear them breathing. Without moving he peered at the room through slits. Then he remembered where he was. Oh my god, what had he done! He picked up his watch from the bedside table. Three fifteen. To stay or leave? To stay, meant the awkwardness of the morning. To leave showed disrespect. He lay there looking at the ceiling.

He decided to go. Zoe had instigated last night and she was a woman of the world. God, the fruit didn't fall far from the tree in this family! He picked up his clothes and crept out of the bedroom. He got as far as the front door and dressed as quietly as he could. As he turned the latch in the door a voice from behind him said.

"Bye Charlie. Speak to you tomorrow."

Startled, all he could do was say "Bye" as he closed the door behind him.

Charlie walked towards his office. Peter was leaning against the door- frame whistling. It was nine fifteen and he was fifteen minutes late to open up.

"Sorry I'm late."

Peter looked at him closely as he put the key in the lock.

"You look like death warmed up. Late night, was it?"

"You could say that!"

"My god, you didn't, did you"?

Charlie went up the stairs without saying a word.

Peter whistled something tuneless behind him.

Charlie reached the top of the stairs, turned and glared at Peter.

"Will you stop that and have some consideration?"

Peter stopped.

"I hope you were considerate last night or it may affect how long we keep this case."

Charlie decided to ignore him and sat behind his desk.

Peter sighed.

"I'll tell you what, why don't you give me a few minutes of your time and then go back to bed."

"Sounds like a plan."

"Right. As I said yesterday, if your sex-ravaged brain can remember, you will need some help in America."

Charlie nodded not wanting to be drawn back to the topic of last night.

"Did you have the time to talk to Zoe about Business?"

"Yes."

Charlie started to feel like he was being interrogated.

"And have we got the go-ahead to spend on a New York agency?"

"Yes."

"OK then. I will start looking on the internet for likely companies."

"You can also look at flights to New York. See what's available."

Peter made a note on his pad.

"And accommodation."

Peter scribbled again.

"Well that will keep me busy this morning, while you are sleeping."

"I'll be back by lunch-time, I just need a couple of hours to clear my head."

"Good. You can bring lunch with you."

Charlie sighed. Didn't see that one coming!

"What do you want?"

"Ham on crusty brown with sliced cherry tomatoes, crispy Cos lettuce, a dash of mustard and mayo."

Charlie looked at Peter

"So that's a ham salad sandwich then."

"Yes but my description sounds more appetizing."

Charlie headed for the stairs.

"And don't forget the donuts."

Charlie went to say something, but decided he may regret it later if he did.

CHAPTER THIRTY

Peter heard the key turn in the lock, and pretended to be asleep in his chair. Charlie reached the top of the stairs saw Peter and threw a packet of crisps at him.

"You don't fool me!"

"Refreshed, are we?"

"Suitably so, thank you."

Charlie sat down on the other side of the desk to Peter and passed him his sandwich. Peter unwrapped it and peeled back the top layer of bread to see the contents.

"So it's a ham salad sandwich then."

"Which by a strange coincidence is what you asked for."

"Are you sure?"

"Yes, you wind up merchant! Anyway what's new in the business world?"

"Well I think I have found you the right agency in New York."

"Who?"

"Well, do you remember the brother and sister who inherited part of Central Park two years ago? She was a private detective and helped the police bring the bad guy to book. They got millions from the City but she still has her agency, all be it more up-market. Now she is a woman who does not need to work another day in her life but chooses to do so."

"So you are telling me she is nuts?"

"No I'm telling you she won't rip you off. She has no reason to do so."

Peter passed a sheet from his notebook to Charlie with the contact details and proceeded to eat his sandwich. Charlie went to do the same, when his mobile rang.

"Hello Charlie."

Charlie felt his colour rising in his cheeks.

"Hi Zoe, how are you?"

"You may well ask. You haven't phoned or called round or anything."

Charlie started to stammer about being busy on the case but was interrupted by Zoe.

"Charlie I was just pressing your buttons, don't worry about it. I just wanted to confirm what we discussed last night, which is to spend what ever you have to. It's all in the will. It's Lily's and my job to see it through."

"OK"

"Good, I have opened a new credit card account in your name for expenses, which should help in America. I have asked for it to be delivered today, by courier. When are you hoping to go?"

"As soon as we have sorted out an American agency to help us."

"You just can't wait to get away from me, can you Charlie?"

"No. No!"

Zoe laughed on the other end of the phone

Then Charlie realised she was winding him up.

"Zoe, you're not playing fair."

"I never said I would. Anyway must go down to Lily and tell her what we got up to last night."

Charlie started to bluster again as Zoe laughed.

"And Charlie?"

"Yes."

"Nine out of ten."

"What?"

"In case you were wondering, nine out of ten. I have to leave you room for improvement."

Charlie's phone went dead.

Peter stared him.

"What are you staring at?"

"A stud."

"Cut it out."

"Now Charlie, be honest, this gives me so many opportunities to pull your leg and I know you wouldn't resent my little pleasures, would you?"

"Sod off."

"Did she score you?"

Charlie coloured up but said nothing.

"She did, didn't she?"

Peter laughed so much he nearly choked on his donut.

"Serves you right."

Peter now had tears rolling down his cheeks.

"So?"

"So what?"

"What was your score?"

"Not a chance. If you think I am going to give you more ammunition, you've got another thing coming."

Peter wiped his cheeks. "Sometimes you are just no fun!"

Charlie looked at the piece of paper in front of him and changed the subject.

"So you think I should phone this Johnson woman then?"

"She looks the best bet to me. If the case intrigues her, she has the background in the police force that could be very valuable to the case."

"Ok I will give her a call."

Charlie picked up the phone and dialled.

CHAPTER THIRTY ONE

Julie sat at her desk in her new swanky offices. So far this morning she had managed just once to get a paper plane through the doorway into the outer office.

Sitting at his desk, Alex was busy at his PC. Julie had taken her nephew on as an intern for the summer, before he went to college.

He was trying to develop forms so they could report their findings to their clients professionally. Easy for them to use and straightforward for the client to read.

Distracted by the pile of paper accumulating in the doorway, he got up and poured two mugs of coffee, taking them through to his aunt's office.

"Explain again why we have no clients?"

"Well it's like this. There are several reasons. Firstly, I moved uptown and upmarket and it takes time to establish a customer base. Secondly because of the publicity about our inheritance, I have a public persona which is detrimental to being a private detective."

She sighed "if things don't pick up I will try to get some referrals from my old police contacts and work up from there. Anyway, how is it coming along with the forms?"

"OK. Come and have a look"

They walked through to the outer office and peered at the screen on Alex's desk.

"That looks good"

"Thanks. You will need a folder to present them in."

"That means art work for the cover, any ideas?"

"I can give it a try, as there's nothing else to do."

"That sort of smart ass talk will take you far!"

"Sorry Aunty"

"Julie, call me Julie around here."

"OK."

The phone rang

They both looked at it like it had landed from another planet.

"Well? Are you going to answer it?"

"Sorry Aunt, I mean Julie."

Julie shook her head and walked through to her office

"One moment please and I will see if she is available."

"Julie, it's a P.I. from England asking for you."

"I don't know any detectives in England! Oh well, put him through."

"Hello, this is Julie Johnson."

"Hello Miss Johnson, my name is Charles Edwards. I'm calling because I need a partner in the U.S., for a case I am working on in the UK."

"What's the case about?"

"Firstly, have you the manpower to start straightaway?"

"Yes but"

"Secondly have you contacts in the law enforcement agencies?"

"Yes but."

"Thirdly what are your rates, daily and retainer costs?"

"Hold on, before we get there I need to know more about you and the case."

"Well Miss Johnson, I run an agency in central England. I'm twenty five years old and an ex police officer like yourself and have been asked to find the Mona Lisa."

There was silence from Julie who thought she had a wacko on the phone.

"In fact, two Mona Lisas!"

"Well I know nothing about art but even I can tell you where one of them is!"

"That would be the fifth, but it's nice that we are already working together!"

Julie laughed "OK so I'm intrigued! What's this all about?"

So Charlie told her.

CHAPTER THIRTY TWO

Charlie put the phone down and looked up at Peter.

"Well she seems interested in the case and said she will start making enquiries right away. So we will see what she can dig up. If you can book me on to the next possible flight, I will go and pack."

"And tell your mother you are going!"

"Oh yes, Mother! Peter I have a favour to ask."

"I don't do favours, but there's a first time for everything"

"Would you cut her lawn for her at the week-end?"

"That's a three pint favour."

"OK."

"I have never met your mother. Is she nice?"

Peter said this with a leer in his voice.

"Behave yourself. That's my mother you are talking about and anyway she would chew you up and spit you out."

"I like a challenge."

"Behave or you will forfeit your beer."

"You know just how to hurt me, don't you?"

Charlie was half way down the stairs and came back so all Peter could see was a head sticking up.

"A courier will be bringing a credit card, so don't leave till I get back."

"Yes O master."

Charlie's head disappeared again as he went down the stairs. Peter shouted after him.

"Bring your passport back with you so I can check you in."

In reply, Peter got an "OK" and a slam from the front door.

Charlie phoned his mother.

"Hi Mom, just to let you know that I will be away for a few days."

"Why?"

"On business."

"Where?"

Charlie was dreading this.

"America"

"What?"

"On business."

"You said that already. So what's it all about then?"

"Can't say but I shouldn't be away more than a week or so."

There was silence for a moment, which Charlie could not take.

"I have arranged for Peter to come round and mow the lawns."

"I don't want a stranger round here."

"Mom, I work with Peter, he's a retired police officer, so be nice to him."

"Tell him not to come before ten or I won't let him in."

Charlie knew his Mom was only taking this attitude because she was afraid for him.

"Mom, it's ok. I will be alright, I promise."

"I can't help but worry about you."

"I know. I will call you when I get back. Peter will be round on Saturday so be nice."

"I will. Take care."

"I will."

Charlie closed his phone and heaved a big sigh.

He got back to the office just before five. The credit card had arrived so he got on the phone and activated it. Peter had found a flight from Birmingham the following morning which they paid for, using the new card.

"So I suppose you want a lift to the airport in the morning?"

"Yes, if you promise not to be too cheerful first thing."

"I will try my best to be a misery in your presence."

"You should email Julie with your arrival time and ask for directions."

Charlie clattered away on the keyboard for five minutes, then turned to Peter.

"I can get the AirTrain from Newark International to New York Penn Station and then get a cab. Seems straight forward."

"You will need some cash."

Charlie looked at his watch. "Better get a move on then."

Charlie headed down the stairs and called back.

"See you in the Acorn in half an hour."

Never one to miss out on a beer, Peter logged out of the computers and headed for the door.

PART THREE

CHAPTER THIRTY THREE
PARIS

He was the eleventh person to hold the post and he was as successful as all those before him. In four years he had achieved nothing of substance. Ramon Ducat, retired police inspector, sat in his office in a ministerial looking building in the centre of Paris and looked around at file-lined walls, most of which he had been through without establishing anything of significance. On his appointment four years ago, the Trustees had explained the heritage of his position.

The letter in his desk drawer from the previous incumbent explained the situation more succinctly.

'To whom it may concern. There is nothing to find. Enjoy the pension.'

The job was for life or retirement. The Trustees could not fire him, he had to wish to stand down from the position. The boredom was soul destroying but the money was excellent. Today was the worst day of the month, second Tuesday, time to face the Trustees and say the same thing he had done for the last four years. "Nothing new to report."

The story goes that the police inspector in charge of the original case, Brunet, became the first incumbent after taking early retirement from the force.

He was haunted by the case and the unanswered questions, which ruined his career.

The former Chairman of the Louvre, Teophile Homille had set up the Trust. After being ousted as a Chairman, he and four other patriotic Parisians felt that the Louvre was hasty in considering the matter closed once the painting was reinstated. The Trustees thought the Louvre commissioners were sticking their heads in the sand. Homille was a man of independent means and had held the position as Chairman because of his love of art and not for the remuneration. He established the Trust to answer the following questions.

What happened to the painting for the two years it disappeared?

Did the thief work alone?

Were there copies produced?

If so who made them?

Where are they now?

And finally Ramon's favourite question.

Is one of them in the Louvre?

After nearly one hundred years, all the questions still needed answering. The Trust had had no direct contact with the Louvre as it was in their interest to dispel any ideas of forgery of its biggest asset. In fact to Ramon's knowledge, they did not know of the Trust's existence.

He gathered up his files and made his way to the committee room to stand in front of the Trustees like a schoolboy who had been playing truant. They felt he had had his opportunity and failed. They wanted results. They wanted him out. The statute stated that the capital investment that ran the Trust would be divided between the existing Trust members when all the questions had been answered. This now ran into many millions of euros. A position on the Trust was inherited, so the members all thought the money in the Trust was their right.

He knocked on the door and entered. The boardroom table stretched out in front of him. The Trustees on each side of the table looking like vultures waiting to pounce. He looked to the far end at the Chairman and went to speak. The chairman's hand rose to stop him.

"We will take it as read that you have nothing new to report, so let me pass on this information."

The chairman gestured to a folded piece of paper on the table in front of Ramon. He picked it up and unfolded it. It contained a name and address in New York.

"Friend of mine informs me that this person has been making inquiries about the painting. You should go and find out why, straight away."

It wasn't a request but an order. Ramon gave a slight nod of his head, turned on his heels and left the room.

The Chairman had brought the meeting to a close and returned to his office. He picked up the phone and pressed a speed dial number.

"He is on his way. I will keep you up to date with his progress and then we will decide what action to take."

"I will be in New York by tomorrow night and awaiting your instructions."

CHAPTER THIRTY FOUR
NEW YORK

Charlie stood on the curb and tried to hail a cab. His flight from Birmingham to Newark had gone smoothly and he had managed to catch up with some sleep. He had taken the train from the airport to Penn Station, the best way to arrive in the middle of it all. A cab pulled to a halt. He swung his backpack off his shoulder and bundled it and himself into the back. He gave the Russian sounding driver the address and relaxed into the seat, taking in the glorious chaos that the streets had to offer.

"Alex, what time are we expecting Charlie to arrive?"

Alex hit a couple of keys on the board in front of him and looked at the screen.

"Peter sent his itinerary through last night. He should be on his way from the airport now."

"Good, make some fresh coffee for our meeting in the boardroom."

Alex smiled. Since moving into the building she had been itching to use their hi-tech boardroom.

"The coffee's primed. The video link with Peter is up and running and I have tested the illustrator so that Peter will be able to see whatever you write up on the screen in a box on his screen alongside his view of us."

"Great. Thanks Alex. I will miss you when you go to college."
Alex squirmed.

Ramon lent against the wall that formed the boundary to Central Park. He was watching the building from the other side of the road. It was one of the smaller edifices along the east side of the park but still a substantial building. Ramon had been in New York for two days and so far had established that Julie Johnson owned the building, having purchased it some eighteen months ago and had the interior remodelled. The brass plaque on the door had three names on it, Johnson Holdings Inc., Johnson Investments Inc. and Johnson Detective Agency. There was a doorman seated inside with the look of a retired police man about him, Ramon could always tell.

The Chairman had passed on the details of the museum and the department that Julie Johnson had contacted and he had gone along to enquire how he would get an old painting appraised.

A young woman met him at the main reception and they had a brief discussion as to how long the process might take. As the conversation drew to an end, Ramon slipped in the only question that mattered to him.

"I bet you get asked for help a lot?"

"Not that often but we did have a lady in here a few days ago asking if we are ever asked to appraise copies of old Masters. Well it was a silly question really because how would you know if it was a copy, if you hadn't had it appraised?"

Ramon offered his thanks and said goodbye.

So here he stood. Waiting for something to happen. No jurisdiction, no contacts, no ideas. But it wasn't winter and there were enough tourists about so that he didn't stand out, so he should be thankful for small mercies. A cab pulled up to the curb and a man got out. Late twenties early thirties, five- ten or eleven, black hair cut neatly. He swung a backpack over one shoulder and pressed the button on the intercom next to the door. An open top tourist bus went past and when it had gone so had the man with the backpack.

He sat on the bed in his Manhattan hotel room. Spread in front of him was a map of New York. He had been here on vacation before but never for work. He studied the map to get a feel for the place and because he may need every advantage that knowledge would give him. The Chairman was happy for him to stay in the comfort of his room and let Ramon do all the legwork. He knew his job was to pick up the pieces, do the dirty work. It was nothing new to him. After leaving the Legion he had made a very good living out of doing other people's dirty work.

Charlie was just thinking to himself that the building was of top quality when the lift doors opened. A lanky teenage boy stood before him wearing the American casual work attire, khaki chinos and a button down check shirt, which was definitely not the boy's choice of clothing. He held out his hand.

"Hi, I'm Alex. Julie's waiting for you in the boardroom."

"Nice to meet you Alex."

Charlie said as he accepted his hand.

"Did you have a good flight?"

"Yes thanks."

Alex took Charlie through a pair of glass doors into the reception area.

"You can leave your pack here."

"OK."

Charlie swung the pack off his shoulder and retrieved a notebook from a side pocket.

"If you would like to freshen up."

Alex pointed towards the toilet door.

"Thanks I will."

Charlie disappeared for five minutes and then Alex led him along a corridor through a single door and on to another pair of opaque glass doors. He pushed one open for Charlie to enter first.

Julie Johnson sat at one end of the boardroom table. As Charlie entered she rose and circled the table to meet him. She was as tall as Charlie, five ten with striking features, accentuated by her short-cropped hair. Pretty with a toned body under shirt and trousers. Charlie could tell by the grace and ease with which she moved that there was a lot of martial arts training in her background. Yet another self-assured independent woman in his life to deal with!

"Hello, I'm Julie Johnson."

Julie took in the man in front of her. Probably in his late twenties, early thirties but with a boyish face that made him look ten years younger at first glance. Dressed in jeans and an open neck shirt and looking like it was his favoured form of dress. His smile on meeting her was open and sincere.

"You must be Charlie. Did you have a good flight?"

"Yes thanks. Managed to catch up on some sleep as well which is always a bonus."

"What would you like to drink?"

"Coffee would be fine. Thanks."

Alex turned towards a side table and poured the coffee for the three of them.

"This case of yours is intriguing."

"Yes it's unusual to be involved in a case that goes back a hundred years. I have been lucky to have Peter to help out, as genealogy is his forte."

"How did you hook up with him?"

"Oh we go back a long way. He was my boss in the police force. He retired and I decided to leave shortly after and start my own agency."

"He is certainly quite a character!"

Charlie coloured up, realising that while he had been in transit for seven hours, Peter had been in conversation with Julie about the case. God only knows what he has been saying! They took their coffee and sat round one end of the table. Charlie thought he would find out a bit more about Julie.

"So how long have you had the agency?"

"About six years. I felt the time was right for me to leave the Force and go it alone. I did quite well through referral work when I first started and I was able to move here earlier this year. You know about the inheritance?"

"Yes. One of your forefathers actually owned a portion of Central Park so you and your brother came into some money from the city and developers. Must have been an extraordinary time for the family?"

"Joe, that's Alex's dad and I have just about started to relax about the money. It was quite a responsibility at first but the rest of the family has been great."

Alex squirmed in his seat.

"Perhaps we should make contact with Peter before it gets too late for him."

Charlie looked at the screen on the wall.

"Looks like you have all the latest technologies."

"Yes. Julie had it installed for just these occasions."

Alex powered up the laptop in front of him and the screen on the wall came to life. A few strokes of the keys later and a face appeared filling the whole screen. The face spoke in a broad Scottish accent.

"Good afternoon to you all, I have gathered you all here today because one of you is a murderer."

Julie and Alex found this all highly amusing.

Charlie looked at the image of Peter on the screen and shook his head.

"I have travelled half way round the world to escape your banter."

"You are such a misery when you are trying to impress someone."

Charlie coloured up.

"I really give up with you."

Charlie knew this was just Pete's way of breaking the ice.

"OK Pete. Give me an update on tracking the paintings."

"The Adams painting. We have an address for the great grandson, one James Adams."

Julie interjected.

"Yes still lives in New York, thought we would pay him a visit tomorrow morning."

"Fine. What about the Parkers?"

Pete coughed to draw their attention back to him.

"Pay attention, class. About an hour ago I spoke to one Tom Parker, the great grandson of Avril Parker. The story goes that one of Avril's daughters upped sticks and went to Hollywood to be an actress in the nineteen fifties. She became the black sheep of the family for leaving the family circle. On his death her father only bequeathed one thing to this daughter, which was announced at the reading of the will. 'A fake for a fake.' So the painting is in Hollywood."

Julie blew out her cheeks.

"The father sounds like he was a real piece of work. Is this daughter still alive?"

"Oh yes and you will never guess who it is!"

They all looked at the screen.

"No guesses?"

Charlie sighed

"Peter, who is it?"

"He only calls me Peter when he is angry with me."

Julie looked at the screen.

"It's a good job you are in another country right now .Who is it?"

Alex had a fit of the giggles at this point, which broke the tension.

"OK then if you don't want to play, it's none other than Teresa Clarke."

The three round the table looked at each other and then back at the screen.

"Who?"

"The young people of today know nothing. She was an icon of the swinging sixties. She was in all the movies that required a girl in a bikini."

Julie looked down at the table, trying not to show she was laughing.

"She made a big impression on you then Pete?"

"Well I wouldn't go that far." His sentence tailed off as he noticed the three faces on the screen in front of him smirking.

"OK, you got me! Yes I did have her poster on my wall back in the sixties."

Now the three faces were all laughing.

Pete looked at his watch, nearly seven.

"That's it. I'm going to get something to eat. I will send you the details for Teresa Clarke and a biog so you will be up to speed. Over and out for now." With that the screen went blank.

Julie looked at Charlie.

"Have we upset him?"

"I doubt it. He is pretty hard to upset."

Julie turned to Alex.

"See what flights are going out to L.A. tomorrow afternoon."

"OK."

Alex got up and went out to his desk in the reception area.

"Well Charlie, have you got somewhere to stay tonight?"

"Pete made reservations for me, somewhere off Time Square."

"We'll tell Alex to cancel them. I have a guest suite on the next floor. Come on I will show you."

"Are you sure? I don't want to put you out."

"You are not! I'm on the top floor in the penthouse."

"Living above the shop?"

"Makes life less complicated, no commute. Come on I will show you around."

They got up and walked back to reception. Alex was already busy trying organize the flight to L.A..

"I'm going to show Charlie the rest of the building and he will be stopping here."

"OK, I will cancel his hotel reservation."

Charlie picked up his backpack and they went up in the lift to the next floor.

"This is the guest accommodation. Let me know if you need anything. You are our guinea pig so there may be odds and ends you need."

"It all looks great to me."

"Leave your bag here and we can continue the tour."

They went up another floor but when the lift doors opened there was no corridor, instead a large open plan living area spread out before them.

"And this is home."

Charlie walked to the panoramic window and just said.

"Wow!"

"It has taken me the last six months to stop saying that myself."

"This is a fantastic place Julie. Now I understand why you want to live above the shop."

"On the first floor are two offices for my holding company and investment company. John looks after all that side of things, and you would have met Ray on your way in."

Charlie remembered the doorman.

"Yes, retired policeman by the look of him."

"You're right. Twenty five years on the force, seen it all, good to have around."

"Good to have a person in that position who can read people and faces."

"Exactly."

"So what did he say about me?"

"I fell in to that one, didn't I?"

"I led you there."

"He said you were ex police and self confident."

"Which is probably what he would say about you."

Julie turned away and looked out of the window.

"Charlie this will be the first case I have tackled since moving here and after years of having to meet my bills every month and watch what I was spending, this all seems such an extravagance, way out of my league."

Charlie nodded but didn't speak. Since his teens people had opened up to him. He didn't know why. One girl in his class said he had an open face and she felt safe in confiding in him. In the police force he was the one called upon when a witness was afraid to make a statement. He would sit in front of them and they would tell him everything.

"I think it's because I am out of my comfort zone and because since moving in, all the excitement has gone."

"While I understand how you feel, I am finding it hard to feel sorry for you. No doubt you are the same person you were and the same investigator, and we all have to live somewhere. You just have to put up with this place."

Julie turned round with a smile on her face.

"That's put me in my place."

"Yes but what a place."

They were both silent looking at the view, then Charlie turned to Julie.

"Tell you what, because you are so kind in putting me up how about I take you out to dinner?"

"That would be great."

"I will let you choose, only remember we are not all made of money."

"Bastard."

Charlie winked at her and turned towards the lift.

"I will go and take a shower. See you in an hour."

He left Julie smiling and shaking her head.

"And I thought Pete was going to be the annoying one!"

As the lift doors closed, Charlie stuck his tongue out at her.

CHAPTER THIRTY FIVE

Charlie stood and let the hot water bounce off his body. He enjoyed flying but the inactivity left him stiff. The heat from the shower was relaxing his muscles and cleared his head. He was pleased that Pete had found Julie's agency. She seemed to be a straightforward sort of person and he liked her. He had been dreading walking into a company with twenty or thirty agents sitting in rows. Feeling that he would be a small client had worried him prior to meeting Julie, but they actually worked on the same sort of cases. He wished he could have an office complex like this, he smiled to himself as he towelled down, it would look a little out of place in Lichfield.

Charlie went up in the lift. It stopped but the doors didn't open. He looked around for a button but there was only a keypad. The doors opened to reveal Julie standing there in a dress and high heels. She looked stunning.

"The doors won't open without the right number, its one seven five two, for future reference."

Charlie thought to himself, remember the golden rule: don't sleep with clients or colleagues. Well he had already broken the first part and would have to play that one out when he got home.

Now all he must do is not complicate the situation over here.

"You look lovely."

"Well thank you kind sir."

Julie gave a little curtsy

"I have booked a table at the best fish restaurant in town for seven thirty, but there's time for a drink before we go."

They walked through to the lounge and Julie poured them both a glass of wine. Dusk was upon them and the view over the park had changed in the last hour. The lights twinkled through the trees and the atmosphere was changing to that of a vibrant night full of the unknown.

"I love the view at this time of night. It brings out the romance of the city but hides the imperfections."

"Very poetic."

"I have my moments!"

They stood with their drinks watching the lights of the city below dance through the trees.

Julie looked at her watch.

"Drink up. We have a cab to catch."

Julie disappeared and reappeared with a coat before Charlie had knocked back the remainder of his wine.

"Come on or the owner will play merry hell with me."

They got into the lift

"So you know the owner, a client?"

"No ex police officer turned detective."

Charlie looked confused

"It's my restaurant Charlie, well mine and my brother Joe's"

They stopped two floors down and Alex got in.

"Any messages?"

"Afraid not."

"Well perhaps Charlie's case will be the start of an influx of new business."

Alex cast his eyes to the ceiling

"Ever the optimist, my aunty."

Julie gave him a flick on his ear.

"What have I told you about calling me that in this building?"

"Ouch! That hurts."

Alex turned to Charlie

"She can be mean so don't get on her wrong side."

Charlie laughed

"I'll try to remember that."

As the lift doors opened Julie tried to flick his ear again but he moved out of the lift too quickly. Ray had seen the lift coming down, so had hailed a cab, into which they all piled. Julie gave the driver the address and they all sat back and relaxed.

The restaurant was at the foot of Manhattan, south of the Brooklyn Bridge, a converted fish warehouse, close to the water's edge. The restaurant itself was on the second floor with kitchens and storage on the ground floor.

As they entered, Joe appeared and kissed Julie on the cheek and shook Charlie's hand

"Nice to meet you."

The restaurant had windows on three sides overlooking the river and the bridge. It was arranged on terraces so that the maximum amount of people could have an uninterrupted view. They went straight to a table in the corner, which offered a view of South Street Seaport. Joe stood by the table with a menu in his hand. Julie knew what was coming.

"Would you like to choose for yourself or can we select a mix of fish dishes for you to sample?"

Charlie looked at Julie

"That's ok with me, if it's ok with you?"

Julie nodded.

Joe turned on his heels and talked to someone who appeared to be the headwaiter.

Charlie turned to Julie who had a smile on her face.

"I'm afraid that one day somebody will want to choose for themselves and Joe will be cut to the quick."

"What about a drink?"

"It's all taken care of Charlie." Charlie laughed

"How long has it been open?"

"About three months and most nights are booked up for the next three months."

"Joe knows what he's doing then."

"Our family has been in the fish business for hundred and fifty years but the restaurant business is very fashion conscious so you have to be on your toes to grab the opportunity. Joe keeps the menu limited on purpose so he can change it with the seasons and availability. "

"It must be a lot of hours for a guy to work when he doesn't need the money."

"Yes, but I have scored brownie points with Kate, Joe's wife tonight by bringing Alex here. It means Joe will have to take him home, so he will get an early night as well."

A waiter appeared with a bottle of chilled white wine on ice and poured two glasses. Julie raised her glass.

"To us Charlie Edwards and our new business partnership."

"To us."

Joe walked up to the table with Alex in tow.

"So you and Kate ganged up on me again!"

"She said she would like to have some down-time with you. I said there was no accounting for taste, but she was adamant so off you go." Joe hoped Charlie would enjoy his meal and bade them good night. Alex followed his dad then turned and said.

"See you in the morning Auntie."

"I get you for that tomorrow."

Alex laughed and waved as they went through the door.

Charlie smiled at Julie

"He seems a very down to earth kid."

"He and his young sister Sarah have done remarkably well in the last twelve months, considering what they went through."

"It must be hard for them to come to terms with inheriting so much money."

"I don't think they have quite grasped the amount involved, but that was the easy part."

Charlie looked at her quizzically.

"Charlie you must not repeat what I am going to tell you. OK?"

"What is it?"

Julie looked around to see if anyone was within ear shot, then moved closer to Charlie and lowered her voice.

"During the negotiations we had some pressure put on Joe and me to sign away the land. We wanted to make sure that any development wouldn't detract from the park, so we wanted some agreement in place to make sure the park boundary was kept in place."

Charlie nodded but didn't interrupt Julie's flow.

"The City and the contractors were under some time constraints so they decided that a kidnapping would speed things up. Only thing was they abducted the wrong target. It should have been Alex, but they grabbed one of his friends by mistake. Joe and I bundled Kate and the kids off to her sister in Newark and I called the police. They called in the FBI on a hunch that the tactic may have been used before in other cities."

Julie took a drink of her wine.

"You know you are the first person I have told since it happened. And I don't know why I am telling you."

Charlie smiled

Julie shook her head.

"That's why."

"What?"

"It's your face."

"What's wrong with my face?"

"Nothing, its just the way you use it."

"That's the strangest thing anyone has ever said to me."

"It's the best I can do. Sorry."

"Anyway, was the boy OK?

"Yes, in the end the police and the FBI managed to work out who it was and get the boy out. A guy from the construction company was behind it and is now doing ten years. They found two other occasions where abductions had taken place and the construction company has set up scholarships for those children. The problem was that we felt responsible for the boy's kidnapping and helpless to do anything about it."

"I can see how you all must have felt. It must be hard for Kate and Joe to let the kids out of their sight, especially as the story has been headlines right around the world now."

"Give me your hand."

"What?"

"Just give me your hand."

Charlie wondered what was coming. Julie took his hand and placed it on the back of her upper arm. Charlie felt a slight raised bump, square in shape.

"What's that?"

"I'm chipped."

"I've heard of cats and dogs being tagged but never humans."

"It's a bit more sophisticated than what is used for pets. After the dust had settled, Joe wanted to insure against the possibility of the kids being kidnapped, so asked me to look into a way of tracking the kids that would be inconspicuous. Once it's implanted and the scar has healed you forget it's there."

"So why have you got one?"

"The kids made the point that we were all vulnerable to kidnapping and wouldn't have the procedure unless we all did."

"So who monitors it?"

"The system is in my office and looks after itself. It plots movements for a seven day rolling period anywhere in the world and has a link to my computer, should there be a malfunction in the system."

"Clever."

"It enables Alex and Sarah to have a normal school and social life without Joe and Kate's fear of not knowing what's happened to them. The chips should last about four years then we will decide whether to have them replaced."

Their food arrived.

Two large platters. One with salads and fries, one containing an assortment of seafood and fish. Charlie didn't realise how hungry he was. He had had nothing since his in-flight meal. The meal was superb, the conversation was limited to discussing the food in front of them. Once finished, they were asked if they would like a sweet, but both declined and settled for coffee.

"So Charlie if we get the Adams' connection sorted out tomorrow, we can be on a plane to L.A. in the afternoon. Have you been there?"

"No. Have you?"

"A couple of times, both on business, but I would like visit on vacation some time. I enjoy all the old films and would like to visit the studios where they were made."

"Sounds fun."

Charlie yawned.

"Sorry, it's not the company."

"I won't take offence. Let's put it down to jetlag and call it a night."

Charlie went to call the waiter over and ask for the bill.

"Charlie what are you doing? I own the joint. You can't pay."

"I said I would buy you dinner."

"You can buy in L.A. tomorrow. OK?"

"OK"

They grabbed their coats and made for the door. They picked up a cab in thirty seconds. Within fifteen minutes Julie was punching in a code on the keypad next to the office front door. When she finished there was a click as the door released and the ambient light in the entrance way brightened. They got in the lift and pressed three.

"You should find everything you need, but if you have a problem press the 'J' on your phone. If you come up for eight thirty in the morning I will sort out some breakfast and we can plan the day. Alex will be here for nine and we can see what flights he can arrange."

The doors of the lift opened and Charlie stepped out.

"Good night and thanks again for the meal."

"You are welcome. Sleep well Charlie."

With that the doors closed and Charlie walked to his room.

CHAPTER THIRTY SIX

Charlie awoke with a start. Not knowing where he was but thinking he was late. He looked at the bedside clock, six thirty. His next thought was that he felt fresh and alert for him at such an early hour, and then it dawned on him that it was the time difference. Now feeling disappointed, he got out of bed, put some coffee on to brew, flicked on a news channel on the TV and got in the shower. After a shave, he dressed and lay back on the bed and watched the breakfast news. His phone rang. Charlie looked at the screen on the mobile, it said Pete. Charlie sighed and pressed the receive button.

"Morning Pete."

"Morning. Did I wake you?"

"No."

"Drats. Oh well you can't win them all."

Charlie said nothing.

"Anyway just to let you know that Zoe phoned and asked after you."

Charlie trying not to rise to the bait.

"That's nice of her."

"Yes I told her you were living with Julie in her big house overlooking the park."

Charlie still not rising to the bait, replied in an uninterested manner.

"Good, I'm glad you told her."

"Look Charlie if you are not going to play the game, how can I have any fun?"

"Pete, it's too early in the morning and I'm going to be late for my breakfast meeting with Julie?"

"OK, I get the message. Pushed aside for two eggs over-easy! Let me know how it's going."

"Will do, we are going to L.A. this afternoon so I will try to give you a call before the flight and let you know how the meeting with James Adams has gone."

"Ok and Charlie, be careful."

With that the phone went dead. Charlie smiled to himself realising that that was why Pete had phoned. Just to say, "Be careful." Old softy!

The lift came to a stop and he punched in one seven five two on the key-pad and the doors opened.

"Come on through." Julie's voice floated from the kitchen area.

Charlie walked around the corner to see Julie sitting at the breakfast bar, drinking coffee.

"Good morning. Did you sleep OK?"

"Yes thanks. Woke early with the time difference so I feel like I've had a leisurely morning already."

"I'll get you some food, I'm sure you are hungry."

"Thanks. I am peckish!"

Julie slid off her stool and busied herself making eggs, bacon and toast.

Charlie sat and watched her cook. He was struck again by her fluidity of movement and her body control.

"You must be quite a yoga expert."

"I wouldn't say expert, but I have my routine every morning and I don't feel that my day is right without it."

"And martial arts?"

"Some."

"I would say you are black belt in at least two disciplines."

"What about you?"

"Some judo at school and a little boxing. But I feel the same way about having a routine only mine involves a pint glass and some beer."

Julie smiled at him.

"You are not fooling me Charlie Edwards. You can handle yourself when you need to!"

Charlie smirked

"I get by."

They ate their food in silence and then Julie put the dishes in the washer.

"I'll get my overnight bag and meet you down at reception. Alex will be here by now."

Charlie went down to his room and picked up his backpack ready for their afternoon flight to L.A.

Charlie got to reception as Julie put the phone down.

"Ray is just hailing us a cab so we had better go."

Charlie said "Hi" to Alex and followed Julie into the lift and down to the street level. Ray wished them both a good morning as he held the front door open for them to pass through. A cab was waiting at the curb. They got in and Julie gave the driver the address. James Adams lived on the upper west side of Manhattan, between the Lincoln Centre and the river.

They were deposited at the entrance of a town house. The front door eight stone steps up from the pavement. Julie knocked on the door. After about two minutes the door opened to reveal a scholarly looking man in his late sixties.

"There you are. You are late!"

He stopped in mid-sentence.

"I'm sorry I was expecting someone else. Can I help you?"

Julie offered her card and asked if they could speak with him for a few minutes.

"How very intriguing, you had better come in."

They were shown into a room containing two pianos and other assorted musical instruments. James Adams sat himself down behind a battered old desk and gestured for them sit across from him.

"I am expecting a student but she is late. I thought you were her. Now how can I help you?"

Charlie let Julie lead the conversation.

"Well sir, we are looking to trace several paintings."

"I'm afraid you have come to the wrong person, I have no paintings."

"The painting we are looking for was purchased by your great-grandfather."

James Adams' face froze, and then broke into a smile, which led to a giggle.

"My my after all these years, I don't believe it!"

"So you do know what we are looking for."

"Oh yes the Mona Lisa."

"We are in fact looking for four."

"Four. My my, well well. Good luck with your hunt but I'm afraid I can only tell you my family story. You see the painting was given away. My ancestor George Adams was a banker and while appearing to be a pillar of the community had his foibles. He had, what used to be called, a wayward eye. He purchased the painting in the first place to placate his wife after one dalliance, then fell for a singer in a speakeasy run by a gangster called Bruno Carboni. Carboni considered the singer to be his property and confronted George. George paid off Carboni and ran off with the singer but not before selling up all the family stocks and bonds converting it to gold and leaving the country. He left some for my great-grandmother, so he must have had some conscience and took the rest with him."

James smiled.

"Three weeks later came the Wall Street crash. So with the worst of motives, he did the best thing for my family in the long term."

Julie shook her head.

"And the agreement with Carboni included the painting?"

"That's right. What he did with it I don't know."

With that the doorbell rang. James got to his feet.

"I hope that I have been of help but that is all I know."

"Most helpful and thank you for your time."

Julie passed him a card.

"Should you think of anything else, please give me a call."

"I will."

As they left as a young girl entered and the door closed behind them.

They could hear the girl being chastised for her "tardy time keeping" as they walked down the steps to the pavement.

Across the street, Ramon Ducat watched them leave and walk to the corner. He decided to follow them as he could always come back and visit the old man later. Crossing the street, he passed behind Julie and her companion who were at the curb hailing a cab just as Julie said.

"We need to talk this through. Let's get back to the office."

Ramon walked to the end of the block and started to hail a cab for himself. As they sat in the cab, Charlie started to ask about Carboni.

Julie gripped his knee and nodded towards the driver. Charlie took the hint and they spent the rest of the trip in silence. Ramon arrived back at Julie's office before they did and took up his position across the street. He watched as they got out of the cab. He used his phone as a camera snapping away at different views including a photo of Julie Johnson and her companion. After they had entered the building he phoned the Chairman.

"They have made contact with an old man who looks to be some sort of teacher."

"What's the address?"

"Why?"

"Simply because if you get killed on the busy New York streets, at least I will have some information."

Ramon gave the Chairman the address.

"I am about to send you a photo of Julie Johnson and her new companion. He appears to me to be ex police, so I am presuming he is a private detective. By his appearance and manner he could be from the UK."

"I will see what I can find out. In the meantime stick with them."

"That was my intention."

The phone went dead.

God, how Ramon hated that man.

They sat round the boardroom table, Pete peering at them from the screen on the wall.

"So how did it go?"

"Well"

Charlie offered the basic facts

"George Adams passed on the painting to a gangster called Bruno Carboni in the nineteen twenties, so we really need to know if his family is still around?"

Julie laughed.

"Oh yes they are still around. Now into running haulage and transport businesses including taxis."

Charlie gave her a knowing look.

"So how do we contact this guy?"

"His name is Richard Carboni and he is one of the wealthiest people in the City. How difficult it will be to get to speak to him is another issue."

"Perhaps an English accent will get us past his secretary."

"Worth a try."

They could see Pete tapping away on his keyboard, finally hitting a command key and the image from his screen appeared on the top corner of their screen on the wall. It showed the home page for Carboni Inc. Listing subsidiary companies, Head Office address and a potted history of the company.

"Well done Pete."

"Glad to be of service."

Julie looked at Alex, sighed then said.

"There is something you should know."

All eyes were on Julie.

"Bruno Carboni may have been responsible for my great great grandfather's death."

Charlie, Pete and Alex stared at Julie.

"You see he was delivering fish to one of the speak-easies owned by the Carboni family when the G men decided to raid. He got caught in the cross fire and killed."

"That's some story."

"Yes. I know it has no bearing on this case but I just wanted to be straight with you both."

Charlie smiled

"So let's try and phone this Carboni."

Charlie read the number off the screen, dialled and waited, listened to the options from the automated voice and he then punched in another number.

"Good morning, I would like to speak to the personal assistant of Richard Carboni please. Thank you."

Alex was giggling at Charlie's upper crust accent. Julie told him to shush.

"Good Morning my name is Charles Edwards, to whom am I speaking?"

"Jordan Taylor."

Julie wrote the name down and Charlie continued his conversation.

"I wish to speak to Mr Carboni on a personal matter regarding a painting that has been in his family for four generations."

Three faces stared at Charlie. He put his hand over the receiver.

"She has put me on hold."

They sat there in silence for what seemed like minutes.

"Yes, that would be excellent. Yes I have the address. That's 2 o'clock then. I look forward to meeting you. Thank you."

Charlie put the phone down.

Julie shook her head.

"You are a con artist, Charlie Edwards."

Pete Laughed

"She's got your number. Will you have time before your flight?"

Alex jumped in.

"Yes, their flight is not until five."

They spent the rest of the morning going through all the information they could find on Carboni. Alex put together a dossier on Teresa Clarke for them to read on the plane. They left for the Carboni corporate offices just after one and from there they would go straight to La Guardia for their flight to L.A.

Carboni Inc. was situated on Hunters Point, just across the water from Rikers Island. The offices were fairly workaday from the outside. Charlie left Julie in the cab, went into reception, which was clean but showing signs of age and asked for Jordan Taylor. He sat for some five minutes and then she appeared through a pair double doors to his left. He smiled to himself, she was beautiful and boy did she know it! Blonde shoulder length hair, high heels, tight skirt. Telling Charlie more about her boss than it did about her. She walked over to where he sat.

"Mr Edwards?"

"Yes."

"Please come this way."

Charlie didn't mind walking behind her at all. Walking back through the doors she had entered, Charlie watched her rear, clothed in its expensive pencil skirt and high heels. It stopped at a lift. She looked over her shoulder hoping to catch Charlie out but he was too quick for her. They went up to the fourth floor. On exiting the lift they had entered another world. This was a top drawer penthouse office suite. It no doubt had all the gadgets, hot and cold running everything.

"Please wait here."

Jordan Taylor gestured to a couch set along a book-lined wall.

"Mr Carboni will be with you shortly."

She turned on her heels and went back to the lift. Charlie watched her disappear and the lift indicator above the doors stop at the floor below. Charlie mused on why a personal assistant would work on the floor below her boss. As Charlie sat, his internal antenna told him he was being watched. He got up took off his jacket, turned around to reassure them that he was not armed, put his jacket back on and sat down. A minute later a door opened opposite where Charlie was sitting and a short wide Italian man appeared. The guy was nearly as wide as he was tall but still managed to mince when he walked. Charlie had never seen the combination before.

"Hello my name is Thomas. Mr Carboni is sorry to have kept you waiting and will see you now."

His broad Brooklyn accent confused with a lisp. Charlie got up and followed Thomas through an outer office doorway, which Thomas had to take one shoulder at a time, and into a large open plan space. Part office, part lounge, and part kitchen. Floor to ceiling glass along one wall gave expansive views of the waterfront, an offshore island and the coastline of the opposite shore of the East River. The person Charlie presumed to be Carboni stood behind a breakfast bar.

"Charlie Edwards, English P.I.. You want a coffee?"

Charlie wasn't sure if it was an offer or a command.

"Please"

"Go sit."

Carboni gestured towards the chairs overlooking the river. Charlie took that as a command and went and sat. Carboni looked as Charlie had imagined. Italian looks, oiled back black hair with just a hint of grey at the temples. He brought the coffee over to where Charlie was seated.

"It is a fantastic view."

"Yeah, that island is Riker's prison. Reminds me every day of where a lot of my forefathers ended up."

Charlie nearly choked on his first sip of coffee.

Richard Carboni gave a little laugh.

"I always start with that line, it breaks the ice."

He laughed again.

"So what can I do for you, Charlie Edwards?"

The emphasis on the 'I' and the 'you' and the use of his full name came straight out of his family background.

"Well you have been checking up on me, so you will presume I am here on behalf of a client."

Thomas stood by the door and giggled.

Carboni looked at him.

"What?"

"His accent is funny."

Carboni shook is head.

"Thomas, go find something to do."

Thomas shrugged and went out the door.

"Sorry about that. He don't get out of the State much. Go on"

Charlie did as ordered. "My client was left a painting in a will. With the painting came a substantial amount of money, which will go to my client should they find the owners of three more paintings. The idea being that if all owners agree, the paintings will be tested for their age."

"Hold on, I'm missing something here, why test a copy of an old picture?"

"Oh I'm sorry. You probably don't know."

Charlie pulled letter from his inside jacket pocket.

"This is a letter sent by the original seller of the paintings to all four original purchasers."

Charlie passed it to Carboni.

Charlie watched as he read and reread the letter, the smile increasing on his face.

"Oh my god!"

"So I can take it from your reaction that you have a copy of the Mona Lisa?"

"Yes. Not here, it's in my place in the Hamptons. You don't know how many times the family has nearly thrown it out."

"I'm glad they didn't."

"So what do you want?"

"Just to know you have a copy and that you are willing to have it tested. It will then be up to the owner of the real one to decide what they want to do with it. I have one more to find then we will be in contact."

Carboni sat shaking his head, "what a thing to leave in a will, the guy must have been nuts."

"In England we call it 'a little eccentric'."

"Thomas, you hear that one."

There came a giggle from a hidden speaker.

"Yes boss."

Carboni smiled at the quizzical look on Charlie's face.

"When you come from a family like mine, the federal government is always trying to get you for the misdemeanours of the forefathers, so nothing goes on in these offices that isn't taped and stored. You may call in a little paranoid."

Charlie couldn't help his response

"Or nuts."

A belly laugh came from the hidden speaker.

Charlie left Richard Carboni his card and Thomas escorted him to the lift doors.

Charlie held out his hand. "Pleasure to meet you Thomas."

"Nice to meet you too Charlie Edwards. The boss won't let me shake hands with people in case I hurt them and they sue."

Thomas waved his hands in a self-conscious manner. They were the size of meat plates. "Yes I know he's a little eccentric."

Thomas laughed at his own joke. The lift doors opened and Charlie stepped in. Thomas put out one of his meat plates to stop the lift doors from closing.

"Next time you come calling bring in the nice young lady waiting for you in the cab. She can have coffee. The boss likes to make coffee."

Thomas smiled and winked, letting go of the lift doors he turned and walked away giggling to himself.

The lift descended and stopped at the floor below, the doors opened and Jordan Taylor stepped in. Without saying a word, she pressed the button for the ground floor. Charlie followed her rear end into the shabby reception area, where she turned this time catching him looking. This amused her just enough to show in her eyes before she stopped an outright smile.

"Thank you for visiting Carboni Incorporated Mr Edwards. Have a nice day"

As she walked back past him, he said, "no, thank you."

She blushed.

Charlie flopped into the back of the cab and Julie asked the driver to pull away.

"Everything OK?"

"Yes."

They headed out on the freeway that would take them across the East River to La Guardia Airport.

Charlie's phone rang. He looked at the screen, number withheld. He pressed the receive button.

"Charlie Edwards."

"Hello Charlie Edwards."

Charlie recognised the lisp.

"Hi Thomas."

Julie mouthed a 'who is it' at Charlie. He put up his hand to placate her.

"Hi Charlie Edwards. My eccentric boss told me to phone you and tell you that you may be being followed by a cab. We don't get a lot of cabs down here. Or my boss is nuts, you choose."

"Thanks for the heads up Thomas."

"No problem Charlie Edwards. Good luck."

Charlie could hear the giggle as the phone went dead.

CHAPTER THIRTY SEVEN

They arrived at the airport and Julie headed for the automated check-in terminal. Charlie stopped her in her tracks. "Let's get a coffee before we check in." She went to object until he gave her a stare. They ordered coffee and found a quiet corner.

"Charlie, are you going nuts? What's going on?"

"I will fill you in on the meeting with Carboni later but his right hand man phoned and said that we may be being followed."

"That's stupid, why would anyone want to follow us?"

"You tell me?"

"Hey Charlie, this is nothing to do with me."

Ramon Ducat followed them to the airport. The cab driver having been well tipped to keep his mouth shut. The stop at Carboni Inc offices confused him. Had it got anything to do with the case? He had no idea.

It now looked like they were on their way somewhere, but he had no idea. They were in the internal part of the departures check-in area, so that narrowed it down to the USA. He was getting heartily sick of the whole escapade. If they used automated check-in he would have no chance of being on the same flight. They were having a cup of coffee, so he found a shop and bought an overnight bag, toothbrush and something to read. He took off his overcoat and put it in the bag. He got there just in time to see them walk towards check-in.

"OK. I'm sorry. It's just that I fail to see how anybody else would be interested."

"Charlie you never know."

"Let's check-in and see if anybody looks out of place."

They stood in the queue and chatted while waiting to move forward.

Ramon saw the board above the counter. L. A., he strolled to the ticket desk and bought a ticket.

Nobody made the hair on the back of their necks stand up. They went up to the departure gate and waited.

Ramon went through to departures and made a call. After two rings an abrupt "Yes".

"Chairman, I am about to follow Johnson and her friend to California, having made a stop on the way to the airport at the offices of Carboni Inc."

"I will find out what I can about the company. The man you are following is a Charles Edwards, private detective from central England."

"Perhaps that is where this all started."

"Perhaps. I will try and get you some information for you on arrival in Los Angeles."

"Thank you."

The phone went dead.

Ramon hated that man.

"Yes Chairman."

"Johnson and Edwards are on their way to Los Angeles, Ducat is with them. Are you going to the address I gave you?"

"Later, about six p.m., early enough to open the door but late enough that I won't be interrupted by other callers."

"You know your business."

"I do."

"Inform me of the outcome as soon as you can."

They boarded the flight on time and settled into their seats. After the safety briefing, people around them started to browse through the in-flight entertainment wearing their ear pieces, which gave Charlie some privacy to tell Julie of his meeting with Richard Carboni.

Charlie's impression of Thomas had the tears running down Julie's cheeks. They had their in-flight meal and drifted into their own thoughts. Both thinking about the possibility of someone following them. Charlie left his seat and walked to the back of the plane. The usual mix of business and holiday travellers. No one stood out as the type to be following them. He got back to his seat and Julie took a walk to the front of the plane. She returned to her seat and shook her head.

"Nothing stood out but if there is a professional following us they wouldn't stand out."

"We will just have to see what happens when we get off."

"We are probably looking for someone on their own. Without any hold luggage. Not too old or too young. So that should narrow it down quite a bit."

"Give it an hour and we can have another stroll up and down the cabin again."

"OK"

They repeated the process two more times during the flight and narrowed it down to about six suited business men. Two in front of them and four behind.

Julie sipped her coffee.

"What's the chance of the person following us having a laptop with them?"

"Next to nil. If they followed us to the airport, they wouldn't have known they were in for a trip until they got there."

"So we can eliminate any of our suspects who have a laptop with them."

"Seems sound to me."

They both read through the report on Teresa Clarke.

"Are you going to get her autograph for Pete?"

Charlie chuckled.

"Yes if the opportunity comes up."

They both became lost in their thoughts and drifted off into a nap.

April Edwards had just finished tidying her make-up when the doorbell rang.

"Hi come in."

As soon as the front door closed, Pete took April in his arms and kissed her. After a few moments, April pushed Pete away.

"There will be time for that later. You have jobs to do first!"

She pointed to the back garden.

Pete shrugged.

"You know I don't like lying to Charlie about us."

"We haven't lied. We just haven't told him the truth, that's all."

"Semantics."

"May be so but I'm quite enjoying having our little secret, aren't you?"

Pete put his arms around April's waist.

"Later, garden first."

Pete pretended to doff his cap and employed a yokel accent.

"Right you are me lady, but I expect the normal payment in kind for my services."

April Edwards laughed and pushed Pete through the kitchen and out into the garden.

Charlie came to on hearing the announcement that they would be landing in half an hour. Julie's head was resting on his shoulder. He liked that she felt comfortable with him enough to do that. Julie stirred, squeezed his arm and went to freshen up.

As the plane came to a stop and the air bridge butted up against the plane, everyone started to collect their belongings and get ready to disembark. Charlie retrieved their bags from the overhead locker and they busied themselves with their bags. This allowed the passengers behind them to move towards the door and for Julie and Charlie to watch them go. Two of the suspects passed with laptop cases, the third with an overnight bag. Something caught Charlie's eye. A little white sticker, no bigger that a fingernail on the bottom corner of the bag. Charlie knew these stickers were used in the production process, when the product was checked and passed to be of a saleable quality. The sticker was in such a position that it would have worn off, if regularly used. So the bag was new. Charlie glanced at the person carrying the bag. Not dressed for L.A. His manner didn't look American. As he went past Charlie turned to Julie and winked.

"So we are at the hotel across the road."

"Yes it's easier that way."

The man passed and went through the cabin door onto the air bridge and out of earshot.

Julie spoke under her breath.

"You see something?"

"Yes, brand new bag and I don't think he is American."

"So you tell him where we are staying?"

"Yes, I want to know where he is."

"Keep your friends close and your enemies even closer!"

"That's the plan."

They walked out of the terminal building and switched on their phones.

They both started ringing in unison. They looked at each other and pressed the button. They both had a message from Alex asking them to phone the office. Julie phoned

"Hi Alex. We just got off the plane."

"Julie you got to phone Sam right away."

"Why, what's wrong?"

"The man you visited, James Adams, he's been beaten-up. Julie he's in a coma."

CHAPTER THIRTY EIGHT

The doorbell rang. That would be David, twenty-five minutes early. Parents often dropped their children off early with the view that they got some free child care time or some extra free tuition. In Joe's case it was for the free childcare. David's mother and father were under no misapprehension that their child would blossom into a real musical talent but as with most parents if they could, they would give their child every opportunity.

James Adams opened the door.

"Joe you are early."

His sentence tailed of as he realised he was confronted by a six foot man and not a four foot boy.

"Can I help you?"

The man didn't reply. Adams knew his mistake was opening the door without looking through the spy hole first. The man smiled at him and the next thing he would remember was being flat on his back in the hallway having had the door pushed at him. His head banged on the tiled floor. He put his hand to it and felt blood. The front door closed quietly and the man stood over him.

"I will be gone in a minute if you answer my questions to my satisfaction."

"What do you want?"

"Your Mona Lisa."

"I do not have the painting."

The man grabbed the front of his jacket and hauled him off the floor, picked him up bodily and dumped him in a chair.

"Where is it?"

"I do not know."

The impact of the slap dislocated the old mans jaw, his denture flying across the room. This seemed to stun the man as much as James.

"Where is it?"

James tried to speak but his bottom jaw wouldn't move. The pain made him cry out. The man got a pad and pen off the desk and thrust it at James. He wanted this man out off his home before David arrived for his lesson. He scrawled Carboni on the paper. The man looked at it and nodded. He pulled James out of the chair and flung him across the room. James landed on the floor and slid into the foot of his desk headfirst, the last thing he remembered as he heard the front door close was that Joe would be safe, and then he blacked out.

They were in Julie's room at the hotel. Once Julie had conveyed the message from Alex, they had decided to check-in and have the privacy of their room before phoning Sam. Charlie had made their tail, seated in the reception area pretending to read a newspaper. He was sure he was right about him and he would find out tomorrow.

"Hi Sam, it's me."

"It's you alright. What have you got yourself mixed up in this time?"

Sam and Julie had been friends since the first day at the academy. Going through basic training together and becoming partners as beat cops. Julie decided to go private and Sam had stayed with the force and made detective grade two years before. Julie had asked Sam to join her in the business last year but she had declined. Julie always suspected that Sam didn't want to jeopardise their friendship by going into business together and the way business had been for the past twelve months Julie was grateful they had stopped as they were.

"Alex told me about James Adams. How is he?"

"Coma, fractured jaw, concussion, cuts and bruises."

"Will he pull through?"

"Too early to say. Anyway it's me asking the questions. That nephew of yours wouldn't tell me anything. What's the case about?"

Julie told her. Then asked.

"So how did you connect me to James Adams?"

"Your business card on his desk. So if Adams didn't have the painting, who has it?"

Julie hesitated to answer.

"Come on Julie, that person may be in danger."

"Richard Carboni."

"Holy shit! You pick'em, don't you? Christ Julie, this could get heavy. You know how long the agencies have been trying to get that family."

"I know but this is a private matter not a business one."

"Don't be naive!"

"You think the FBI is going to get involved if they hear about this? You better believe it."

There was silence while they both thought about it.

"Should I phone Phil?"

Phil was the lead agent in the kidnapping case involving Julie's family.

Sam sighed

"No leave it to me. I will try to keep them out of it as long as I can. So how's this good looking P.I. from the UK working out?"

"He's working out fine and listening to every word you say."

"Oh good. Hi Charlie, she's got loads of money and a hell of a figure if she has a mind to show it off."

Charlie laughed.

"And a hell of a mind too!"

"Hey Julie he sounds like a keeper."

"Bye Sam."

Julie went to close the phone.

"And Julie, have a nice time in L.A. and keep me up to speed."

"Will do."

Julie closed her phone.

"What's the problem with the FBI involvement?"

"As a private investigator you can afford to be a little sketchy with the truth when talking to the police, protecting your client and sources if you think it will help the case you are working on. If the FBI take an interest they take over and you are out of the game until they say so. They have been known to lock people up for obstruction. The police threaten to, but rarely do."

"I see, so why didn't you tell Sam what we are doing in L.A.?"

"She didn't ask. And the reason she didn't is because she didn't want me to give her a half-truth. She knows I will keep her in the loop as and when she needs to know."

"Any news of James Adams?"

"Not really, he is in a coma and they don't know if he will pull through."

"Why beat up an old man? It doesn't make sense."

"We think that we are being followed. James Adams gets beaten up and we are going to visit the ageing Teresa Clarke tomorrow."

"We will have to be careful Julie. If we have caused James Adams to be in a coma because we visited him, we have to cover our tracks tomorrow."

Julie picked up the bedside phone and spoke to reception.

"Could you organise a medium size rental car for me to collect at nine am in the morning?"

Julie put the receiver on the cradle.

"That's sorted. You will go by cab and I will follow behind in the rental. If anyone is following you, I will see them."

"Sounds good to me."

Charlie sighed

"I have to make a phone call that's going to be awkward."

"Carboni?"

"Yes."

Charlie got his phone out and scrolled to 'received' calls, found the last number and pressed dial.

"Hello Charlie Edwards."

"Hello Thomas."

"The boss is in a meeting, you want to leave a message?"

"Yes Thomas. You know that we got Mr Carboni's name from James Adams?"

"Yes I overheard the conversation."

Thomas gave a little giggle.

"Well somebody beat him up. He's in hospital in a coma."

There was silence on the other end of the phone so Charlie continued.

"It may not be related but I thought you should know."

Thomas became all business.

"You haven't told the police of your visit here?"

"No."

"Do you think it was the person who may have been following you when you came here?"

"We think he travelled with us to L.A."

"So there could be two people involved."

"Possibly"

"Jesus, Charlie Edwards, you know how to spoil my day, the boss will go ape over this."

"Well he is a little eccentric"

Thomas did not giggle

"Sorry Thomas, but as I said it may not be related but I thought you should know."

"You did the right thing Charlie Edwards. Don't get sunburnt out there."

"Thomas before you go, the guy you thought was following me, did you get an image of him?"

"Charlie Edwards, no one gets within a quarter of a mile of this office without we don't know what they look like."

"Can you describe him to me?"

Julie waved across the room at Charlie.

"Ask him to email it to us."

Charlie passed on the address and said good-bye.

Julie was already opening her laptop.

"This will prove if we are good little detectives or just paranoid."

Julie opened the mail and they both stared at the image and smiled at each other.

CHAPTER THIRTY NINE

They both slept well in their respective rooms and Julie ordered breakfast for two in her room so they could talk through their plan for the day.

"I had a thought last night."

"Didn't your mother tell you that was bad for you?"

"Very funny! We need to know who is behind this and we can only start with the people who knew about my visit here."

"Your clients, me and Alex, you and Pete. Perhaps your clients are trying to eliminate the other paintings?"

"That only works if they know their painting is the original and if they do they don't need to eliminate the others. It wouldn't hurt to dig a bit deeper though."
Charlie looked at his watch.

"Pete will be in the pub right now, so let's send him an email he can work on when he gets to the office in the morning."

They finished their breakfast.

"It's time to collect the car. You OK with the plan?"

"Yes. I'll stay here till you are on your way and give me a call."

Julie picked up her bag and made for the door. As she went through it she turned back.

"No heroics Charlie. That's what you are paying me for."

Charlie realised Julie had gone into business mode and wasn't about to argue with her.

Julie went to the reception desk and made a deal out off signing for the rental car, then headed through the front door absent-mindedly rattling the keys in her hand.

Ramon Ducat put down the paper he was pretending to read and followed her outside. This was his worst nightmare, them splitting up, but he felt he had to follow the one on the move. He watched Julie Johnson find her car in the section of the car park allocated to the rental company.

He asked the doorman to hail a cab. One pulled up just as she pulled out into the street. He dived in the back and asked driver to follow at a distance. The driver said something in Russian but proceeded to follow.

Julie saw the cab pull out in her rear view mirror and phoned Charlie.

"He took the bait."

"OK. I'm on my way."

Charlie went down to the front of the hotel and picked up a cab. He gave the address to the driver and they pulled away. They had used an Internet mapping system to find a location that would be quiet and be a reasonable distance from the hotel. Charlie arrived in the quiet residential street in Hollywood ten minutes later. Pulling to the curb, the driver asked for the fare.

"I am waiting for someone to join us, so keep the meter running."

"OK. You're the boss."

Charlie phoned Julie.

"I'm in place."

"OK, Five minutes."

Charlie told the driver they were meeting someone in another cab in about five minutes. The driver shrugged his shoulders.

"You're paying."

Shortly after Julie sailed past and took a left turn. A minute later a cab went past them and took the left turn.

Ramon asked his driver to pull into the curb after they had turned the corner as he could see Julie had pulled on to a driveway one hundred yards ahead. At first the cab pulling up behind him didn't register, as he was wondering why Johnson hadn't got out of the car. Then it was too late. The rental spun its wheels as it reversed off the drive. The front of the car swung round in a screech as the tyres fought to grip the road and then accelerated towards the front of the cab.

Ramon's cab was now sandwiched between the rental car and Charlie's cab. His Russian driver pulled a baseball bat from under his seat.

Ramon flopped back in his seat.

"You won't need that. How much do I owe you?" The driver told him but still held on to the bat. Ramon paid and resigned himself to the fact that he had been made, so he had to face the music. The cab door unlocked and he opened the door and got out. As he did, Charlie got out of the cab behind and the driver reversed away, then did a u-turn and spun his wheels as he drove away. Ramon's cab did the same, nearly knocking Charlie over in the process. Julie lent across and opened the passenger door and beckoned Ramon to join her. He didn't see the point in offering resistance as he was a retired police officer and they were both young and could out run him any day. Charlie got in the back and Julie pulled away from the curb. Ramon thought he would cooperate within reason so offered his name.

"I am Ramon Ducat, formally of the French police force, now retired."

"You know who we are and you know what we are doing here."

"Yes you are trying to find the owners of the copies of the Mona Lisa."

"And you are following us. Why?"

"Because the people I work for want the copies."

"And possibly the original?"

"The original is in the Louvre, is it not?"

Ramon's smugness got to Julie. She pulled to the curb and pulled her gun out of her bag and jammed the barrel into Ramon's thigh.

"I am a reasonable shot but not good enough to say I would miss your femoral artery if I squeezed the trigger right now."

Ramon went as white as a sheet. Charlie was taken back by the speed in which she had acted, but played along.

"Monsieur, I would suggest you answer her questions."

Ramon's composure was coming back.

"You would not shoot me in broad daylight."

"Don't tempt me, there is a lot of car-jacking in this area and as I am an ex police officer, my story will be believed by the police here. Don't make me waste a bullet."

Ramon raised his hands.

"OK."

Julie put the gun away.

"Right who are you working with?"

"I am here on my own."

Julie reached for the gun in her bag.

"There's no need for that! I am telling the truth."

Charlie jumped in from the back seat.

"Did you follow us to James Adams' home?"

"I do not know the name. Is he the old man with the steps to his house?"

"Yes."

"Yes I did."

"Did you know he is in hospital, in a coma?"

"No, but that has nothing to do with me."

As he spoke the words, Ramon wondered if the Chairman was playing him. Julie saw a glimmer of realisation in his eyes.

"What is it?"

"I report to a man in Paris. He could have passed the information on to someone else."

"Who?"

"I really do not know. Did this James Adams have anything stolen?"

Julie recognised it, as a question a police officer would ask.

"Not that they could see. His jaw was dislocated and his skull cracked."

"I am sorry if I brought this to his door but I have no knowledge of the attack."

"So what are you supposed to do?"

"Simply let you lead me to the people who have the copies and then try and obtain them."

"By any means?"

"No I wouldn't want to be involved in anything inappropriate."

"So who do you work for?"

"It is hard to explain."

"The Louvre?"

"No, they have no connection with the Trust."

"The Trust?"

Ramon explained about the history of the Trust and why each generation wanted to fulfil its obligation and reap the rewards.

Charlie puffed out his cheeks.

"So this has been going on for a hundred years all because the Chairman of the Louvre got the sack when the painting was stolen."

"The first members of the Trust didn't feel a carpenter could have been the mastermind behind the theft and that they felt the Louvre was too happy to accept the returned painting as genuine."

Julie not one to miss the point.

"So how much is in the bank balance for the Trust today?"

"I do not know but it must be several million euros."

"It's always money or sex."

Ramon shook his head.

"It is the same the world over."

"How did you find your way to New York?"

"The Chairman gave me the tip that someone had been making enquiries at the Metropolitan Museum."

Julie shrugged

"That would have been me."

Silence descended in the car as they all started thinking things through.

Charlie spoke, "let's get back to the hotel."

They drove in silence, Ramon gripping his seat belt because of Julie's aggressive driving style.

Charlie remarked as they drove.

"You can take the girl out of New York but you can't take the New York out of the girl!"

They sat in the coffee shop of the hotel and went over what they had discussed in the car. Julie led the conversation in a way that Ramon did not appreciate. She doodled on the pad in front of her and asked the questions in an absent-minded fashion.

"So you are tasked by the 'Trust' to find the copies of the Mona Lisa and to establish if one of the copies is the real thing."

"Yes."

"You are employed by the Chairman, whose name is?"

"I don't know."

"So you expect us to believe that you have worked for the Trust for four years and in that time you never took it upon yourself to find out who you work for?"

"You don't understand, it is part of the agreement that we do not search out the names of the Trust members. If we are found to have done so, our contract is terminated."

Charlie smiled and joined in the discussion.

"So it really pays well?"

"Yes, better than a pension."

Now Julie was smiling.

"So to comply with the Trust rules they have to employ someone and you do it because it pays well and you don't have to do anything."

"Up till now."

"If we believe you, that you thought that you were working alone and that you no longer want to be associated with the Trust, will you phone the Chairman and tell him what we ask you to?"

"I am still well paid by them, what would be my compensation?"

Julie's face turned to stone. She spoke quieter than Charlie had heard her before.

"We will not take you to the police. We will not say that you are complicit in a brutal attack and I may not shoot you in the leg."

Ramon looked at Charlie.

"Is she always this direct?"

Charlie gave a little laugh

"Yes it's the New York way, but personally I would have arranged for you to fall down the flight of stairs, then I am from England and we tend to do things a little differently. The outcome would be the same. You would probably have trouble walking again."

Ramon went white as a sheet for the second time that day.

"OK. You will have my cooperation."

Charlie held out his hand towards Ramon.

"Give me your phone."

"What if the Chairman should call?"

"You can only speak to him in our presence."

Ramon looked forlorn.

"And your passport and credit cards."

Ramon went to protest and then gave a Gaelic shrug and emptied his pockets. Charlie picked up his room key and looked at the number. He opened the wallet, taking out the cards and all the bills.

"Good. Now you have the run of the hotel while we have an appointment to keep. On our return you can phone the Chairman with some information."

Ramon picked up the key and stood up.

"I will wait for your return in my room."

With what dignity he could muster he walked towards the lifts.

They watched him enter the lift and then both burst out laughing.

They drove into old Hollywood, with its palm lined streets and art-deco inspired houses. Tourist trams were the only other traffic. With their passengers' heads turning left and right as the tour guide pointed from one house to another. They turned off the main drag into a narrower cul-de-sac, built in the nineteen fifties. All the properties were of differing designs but of a similar size. Charlie spotted the number of the one they wanted and they pulled on to the driveway.

They rang the doorbell. Two minutes later a man, in his late sixties or early seventies, opened it. He was wearing a pair of tailored shorts, polo shirt, rope soled sandals, a sea captain's cap on the back of his head and the butt of a cigar in the corner of is mouth, his skin like polished leather. Julie made the introduction and asked if it would be possible to see Teresa Clarke.

"Sure why not? Come on in." They entered a sprawling house, all built on one level. He led them through the lounge, designed in the sixties and still like new, all pastel colours and deep pile rugs.

"She's outside, potting out some plants."

Walking out on to the patio, they could see a woman bent over a planter. She was wearing white peddle-pushers, canvas sneakers and a light blue, tailored man's shirt, tails out, with the cuffs rolled back to just below her elbow. She turned at the approaching footsteps. Tall and willowy with her blonde hair tied back in a ponytail. Her skin a contrast to Al's, pale but with a glow to her cheeks.

"Hon, we got guests."

"I can see that. Who the hell are you?"

Julie made the introductions.

"OK. So what do you want?"

Charlie explained that they had spoken to her nephew and they were interested to know if she still had the painting.

Teresa Clarke pointed to the table and chairs by the side of the pool.

The guy in the cap remained standing.

"Don't loiter Al, go make some iced tea."

Al shrugged and walked away.

Teresa watched him disappear in to the house.

Julie remarked

"Seems a nice guy."

"I only keep him around for the sex. He's got money too. My husband died fifteen years ago and Al has been a comfort, if you know what I mean."

Charlie thought they needed to get back on topic before they were offered too much detail. He explained about the will and hoped that Teresa would be happy to have her painting tested.

"You mean to say that the fake my father gave me could be the real thing?"

"Yes, a one in five chance."

She started to laugh and then the laughter turned to tears.

Al reappeared with the iced tea.

"Hey, what have you been saying to her?"

He went and put his arm around her and gave her a squeeze and stroked her hair.

"I think you had better leave."

"Al, it's OK. They aren't responsible. It's my father."

Al looked bewildered and looked at Charlie for an explanation. Charlie explained and Al burst out laughing.

"The old buzzard would be turning in his grave if he knew."

Teresa composed herself and poured the tea.

"So what happens now?"

"Well we are on our way back to New York tonight and then Charlie will be on his way back to the UK."

"Yes. You will be contacted by the lawyer in charge of the Estate to arrange for your painting to be tested. I have no idea how long the analysis will take to process but we will let you know the results as soon as we can."

Julie had a question.

"Do you have the painting here?"

"No it is in storage. I can't bear to look at it, but I can't throw it away either."

"That's understandable."

They sipped their tea and Charlie asked.

"Is it possible to have an autograph for my associate Pete back in England? He is a real big fan of your films."

"Let me guess, he was in his teens in the sixties?"

"That's right."

"Horny as hell, had my picture on his bedroom wall?"

Charlie and Julie started to laugh.

"Right again."

"I could turn men to jello in my day."

Al lent across and kissed her full on the mouth.

"Hon, you can still do it today."

Julie looked at Charlie and gestured that they should leave.

They made their excuses about catching a flight and walked to the front door with Al. As Al opened it, Teresa reappeared with a large envelope.

"This is for Pete's eyes only. Don't open it."

"Thank you very much. I'm sure he will appreciate it."

"Oh, I know he will."

CHAPTER FORTY

On the way back to the hotel they discussed the conversation Ramon should have with his boss and decided to tell Ramon that their meeting had only pointed them back to New York, as the painting had been given as a present some years before. They made a list of points for him to raise. They both had a smattering of French but Charlie had a better understanding so would listen in on the conversation.

They knocked on Ramon's room door. They heard movement inside and then the door open.

"Was your visit fruitful?"

"Not exactly, but it will send us back to New York."

"Is that the truth or is that what you want me to tell the Chairman?"

"We are going back to New York tonight."

"OK."

Charlie produced Ramon's phone and passed it to him together with the list of questions they wanted answers for.

"If I ask all these questions, he will become suspicious of me."

"So which ones are you comfortable asking?"

Ramon looked at the list.

"This,this and this."

"OK. Start with those questions and see how the conversation progresses. Remember you followed us to the house and questioned the owner, a retired actor, about the painting and he said it was in New York, which you will follow up on your return."

Ramon found the speed dial number and called. It was answered after the first ring even though it was night in France.

"I have been waiting for your call."

Charlie had his head next to Ramon's, so he could hear the conversation.

"It has been difficult but I will be returning to New York tonight."

"And you found the painting?"

"No but I know that it is in New York, given to an actor as a present."

"Very well, give me the address."

Ramon gave the address on the sheet of paper. Julie smiled, as she knew it was the address of a cemetery.

Charlie tapped the paper at question one and Ramon nodded.

"Have you a name for me of the old man they visited? I will call on him on my return."

"Call me when you get to New York and I will decide what action I want you to take."

"And Carboni Inc?"

"Again I will contact you when you are in New York."

Ramon's face coloured up.

"Is there something you are not telling me Chairman?"

"Only that you are trying my patience."

With that the phone went dead.

Charlie pulled away from Ramon.

"He must pay you a lot."

"It is not enough."

Julie asked what had been said and Ramon told her with Charlie nodding in agreement.

"Sounds a real piece of work!"

Ramon shook his head.

"What else can I tell you?"

Julie gave a knowing smile to Charlie who answered.

"The address of your office in Paris and anything you think will help in finding out more about the 'Trust'."

Ramon wrote down the address and passed it to Charlie.

"OK. We need to send an email and book ourselves on a flight this evening."

Charlie held out his hand.

"Phone please."

Ramon handed over the phone.

"Sorry but people's lives may be at stake and until we can trust you completely, we will carry on the same way."

Ramon shrugged.

"I would do the same."

They left Ramon in his room and went up a floor to Julie's.

They emailed Pete and asked him to find out what companies had offices in the building at the address Ramon had given them and also asked him to find the descendants of the Chairman of the Louvre at the time of the theft. Julie sent a message to Alex saying they would be back in the morning.

Within an hour they were walking across to the airport. They boarded their flight on time and settled into the long flight.

He had had his orders from the Chairman. See if the painting is there, if it isn't then try and establish where it is. The difficulty was that this wasn't a private dwelling but an office block, so more care would be needed. He had spent the previous night watching the rotation of the guards and had a window to gain access. He had studied the building from all angles and concluded that Carboni had his offices on the top floor and possibly lived there, as he hadn't appeared to leave. He had prepared as much as he could and yet here he sat manacled to a chair with cable ties. A large man sat in front of him, staring at him.

"No harm will come to you if you answer my questions. Why have you broken in to these premises. Who do you work for?"

He had no intention of talking so stared back at the man with the lisp.

"You are not American."

Not exactly a question more a statement, but he gave no indication of confirmation. He just stared at the big man. He was still going over in his head what had happened to put him in this situation. Was he slipping? He knew that wasn't possible.

The large man suddenly got up and left the room. The camera in the top corner of the room had its little red light on, they were watching him.

The phone rang twice.

"Hi boss it's me. This guy isn't going to give us anything without help. Do you want me to help him?"

"He knows how to handle himself?"

"My guess is some sort of special forces."

"OK. Have fun but make sure you clean up after yourselves."

"No problem boss, speak to you later."

Thomas turned to the woman sitting next to him.

"Jordan, you don't have to be involved in this if you don't want to be?"

"Uncle Thomas, this man came after my father. I would like to deal with the matter."

Her Boston accent, a clue to her schooling.

"OK. but if you need help I will be watching."

Jordan Taylor entered the room.

"I will presume that you speak perfect English so please pay attention. There will be some great discomfort to you but the amount is purely down to your cooperation."

Jordan signalled to the two men standing by the door. They dragged the chair containing the man to the side of the room. He looked slightly bemused. They then spread a plastic sheet across the floor and lifted the man in the chair in to the middle of the sheet. Jordan, dressed in tailored trousers and boots, proceeded to put on a pair of coveralls and a baseball cap.

"Not the best designer outfit I have ever worn but they are disposable. Right shall we start?"

Thomas watched on the monitor and couldn't have been more proud if it had been his own daughter. Thomas could see the colour rising in the man's cheeks, Jordan had his attention.

"Who are you working for and why are you here?"

The man just looked at Jordan.

The blow was to be expected but the power was not. Jordan took two strides towards the man and thrust a straight arm, the heel of her hand sinking into the base of his sternum. The force broke the bottom left hand rib with an audible crack. He gasped for air as the pain shot across his chest. Jordan went and stood behind the man in the chair. Shaking her wrist out she looked at the camera and mouthed 'ouch'.

"We can play pick a rib if you like. You say which one you want me to break next and I guarantee to do it."

Silence was the only reply. Jordan slapped the man across the ear. Cupping her hand as she did it and then flattening it out on impact. The air pressure on the inner ear perforated his eardrum, extracting a yelp of pain. Jordan bent down and whispered in his good ear.

"It's OK. I won't do that to your other ear."

The man was now rolling his head from side to side. Jordan walked round and stood in front of the man.

"Who are you working for and why are you here?"

Silence. Jordan stamped on his left foot with her high heel boots. The force broke his third and fourth metatarsal. He screamed.

As he settled, Jordan looked at her watch.

"Well, we have only been together for five minutes and you have two or three broken bones and a perforated ear drum."

She stamped on his other foot. This time there was a snap followed by a yelp of pain. Jordan walked around the back of the man and with all her power chopped down on the top of his shoulder. At first she thought she would just bounce of his well-built frame but her power told again, causing nerve damage to his right arm.

Jordan walked round to the front of the man in the chair and bent down in front of him.

"You are determined to take your secrets to the grave. Surely that is not worth the money you are being paid."

Silence. Jordan turned to one of the two men standing by the door.

"Is the boat ready and the weights in place?"

"Yes."

Jordan shook her head at the man in the chair.

"I will be back in a moment."

Jordan left the room. The man had trouble holding his head up and continually squirmed with pain.

"What do you think, Uncle?"

"We found his rental car and his hotel room key, the details of where he is staying were on the paperwork in the glove box. I have someone looking at the room now."

"What about him?"

They both looked at the man on the screen in front of him.

"Well Jordan Taylor, you did a good job in proving that this man has been trained to withstand this sort of treatment and ain't going to crack until the end game."

"OK."

Jordan Taylor picked up a large plastic bag off the table and re-entered the room.

"We have your car and your room key. Someone is in your room right now, so we will be able to find out what we want in time. So I have no need to waste time with you."

Jordan turned to the two men in the room.

"You can leave now and turn the camera off."

They left and the red light on the camera went out.

Jordan made a big show of opening the bag and then walked behind the man in the chair placing the bag over his head.

"Wait"

Jordan pulled the away.

"Yes?"

"I answer to the Chairman. I do not know his name. I am here for the Mona Lisa."

"How do you contact this Chairman?"

"I do not, he contacts me."

"Then as we have your phone, we will await his call. You have been misled. There is no Mona Lisa here."

With that Jordan Taylor placed the bag over his head and pulled it tight. She gathered it in one hand and twisted it. With the other hand she produced a hypodermic, pressing the needle in to the side of his neck. The man went limp.

The door opened and Uncle Thomas came in applauding loudly.

"You are a true Carboni!"

They both laughed. Thomas produced a knife and cut the cable ties. With one motion he heaved the man on to his shoulder and edged through the door.

"Back in thirty minutes."

Thomas walked as if he wasn't carrying anything. Out through the plant room door and down to the water's edge. He dropped the man into the back of a small motor launch and then got in the front. In ten minutes he was at South Brother Island. He lifted the man out of the boat and stuffed a note down the front of his tunic.

The note read.

'We had fun. Do drop by again and we can show you some more of our party games.'

CHAPTER FORTY ONE

Alex had coffee and pastries waiting for them when they got back to the office. They had allowed Ramon to go to his hotel and shower. He said he would return in an hour. Charlie and Julie did the same and they all met up in the boardroom. Alex had established the link with Pete and they sat exchanging information.

"Charlie I mowed your mother's lawn. Nice woman, your mother."

"Pete, I told you to behave."

"Your mother doesn't need protecting from me you know."

"Fine"

"Well OK then, I traced the address in Paris that Ramon gave you. Contains four firms of lawyers and one of them owns the building."

"And who runs that business?"

"One Theophile Homille, no less. And before you ask, yes it is the same name as the director of the Louvre when the painting was stolen."

Julie turned to Ramon

"So now you know who you are working for."

Ramon shrugged

"So what do we do now?"

Charlie's phone rang.

"Is that you Charlie Edwards?"

"Yes Thomas, it's me."

"We had a visitor last night, thought you might like to know."

"Is everybody alright?"

"Yeah, the boss went up to the Hamptons so Jordan and I played host for the night."

"Jordan?"

"Hey Charlie Edwards, don't underestimate my niece. She can have fun with the best of them."

Charlie made a mental note to find out who a girl was related to before he started flirting.

"So anything new from your visitor?"

"Yeah, his name, his hotel room, nationality."

"He's French, right?"

"Ha Charlie Edwards, you been detecting?"

Thomas gave a little giggle

"He calls his boss the Chairman."

"Now you just showing off!"

"Have you got a name for this guest of yours?"

"I'll email you what I got, photos and all."

"Thanks Thomas. Sorry if your guest was inconvenient."

"No problem, it was fun. Bye Charlie Edwards."

"Thomas before you go, is your guest still around?"

"Yeah, he's somewhere but he probably got stiff muscles this morning from dancing too hard. Bye Charlie Edwards."

The Phone went dead.

All the faces around the table looked at Charlie.

Julie spoke.

"So how is your gangster friend?"

"He had a visit from our mystery man last night and to put it in Thomas's parlance 'they entertained him'. He is going to send us the info he got out of him."

Julie looked a little concerned. Charlie smiled at her.

"Don't worry the guy is still alive."

Alex looked down at his laptop.

"We have a message."

"He transferred it to the wall screen."

They all read it.

"Henri Le Saux, well that's what's on his passport."

"Pete, could you try and find out what you can about this guy? We know he is French and we know he has had military training to a high combat level."

"Yes and he is a mercenary, so he may have been kicked out for some reason."

"Ok. I will get on with it and let you know."

Charlie thought of something and laughed

"You know that with all that's been going on, I forgot the main issue!"

They all looked at Charlie.

"Pete, would you like the pleasure of phoning Lily and telling her that we now have traced all the paintings and in principle all are in agreement to have their paintings tested?"

"It would be my pleasure. Speak to you later."

"OK. Ramon do you want to phone the Chairman and let him know you are back in New York?"

"Yes, see what he expects me to do next."

Charlie gave Ramon his phone and sat next to him while he called.

"You are back in New York?"

"Yes."

"I have decided that we are getting nowhere and that the root of this investigation starts and ends with that investigator Charles Edwards. I am on my way to England to try and find out who is responsible for hiring him. That is where we will get the answers that I am looking for. He is based in Lichfield, in the centre of the country. Join me there as soon as you can."

The phone went dead.

Charlie turned to Alex.

"Can you get Pete back?"

"Yes of course."

Julie looked concerned

"Charlie, what's wrong?"

Ramon answered.

"The Chairman is going to Lichfield."

As he said it, Pete's face appeared on the screen.

"I know I'm fast but not that fast!"

Pete saw the expression on Charlie's face.

"What's going on?" Charlie told him.

"Pete, I want you to get Lily and Zoe to go away for a few days."

"What about your mother?"

"Why Mom?"

"Charlie if they are as desperate as they appear to be and they want to get to you, they may go after your mother."

"You are right. If this Henri Le Saux is still in the game, he is probably on his way to Lichfield as we speak."

"I'm shutting down now, call you later."

With that the screen went blank. Charlie turned to Alex.

"Could you get me on tonight's flight back to Birmingham?"

Ramon raised his hand

"And me"

Then Julie raised her hand.

"You had better make that three."

Charlie looked at Julie and smiled.

"You are not leaving me behind!"

He always made a habit of befriending the chambermaid when stopping in a hotel. You never know what you are going to need.

"Hi, I seem to have lost my key card, must have left it in my room."

"No problem, it's strange that it's always the men who lose their keys."

"Ah that's because we have no handbags to carry our belongings in!"

She opened the door

"Have a nice day."

"Thank you. You too"

He shut the door behind him and nearly collapsed on the floor. The pain was bad enough but pretending not to be in pain made it worse. After coming to on that island, he had managed to hail a boat, which dropped him on the Manhattan shore. He walked south and then east and found Central Park. Then stumbled his way down the length of the park and finally back to his hotel.

He undressed and sat in the bath with the shower on full. The heat easing some of the pain. He took stock. The ringing in his ear seemed to alter depending on which way he turned his head. The feeling in his arm had come back but still felt sore. His ribs only hurt when he breathed heavily. But the worst were his feet. They were both black and blue and lying there in the bath he could have sworn he could see them swelling before his eyes. He needed tape them up, otherwise he wouldn't get his shoes back on. He hauled himself out of the bath and gingerly dried himself.

Only then did he notice the state of his room, someone had been through it and wanted him to know they had. It was a mess. He panicked for a moment, sliding back the wardrobe door and feeling above the door. It was still there where he had wedged it, a safe deposit key. He had done the same thing at every hotel he had stayed in for the past ten years, but this was the first time he would have to use his back up papers. He wondered if he was getting too old for this or just careless.

Dismissing both thoughts he dressed and went down to reception and asked for his box. The receptionist showed him into a side room so he could have some privacy. Everything was there. Spare room key, passport, phone, credit cards and cash. He went to the lobby shop and bought four rolls of surgical tape, some pain killers, a large coffee and a Danish. He went back to his room, taped his ribs and feet, lay on the bed with his coffee, Danish and pain killers. He rang the Chairman.

"I ran into some trouble last night and didn't establish where Carboni has the painting."

There was silence on the other end of the phone.

"I'm sorry not to have completed the task."

"It is of no matter now. I need you in England. I believe the beginning of this situation is where we will find the answers and that is with Charles Edwards' original client."

"I will get on the next flight and call you when I arrive."

He phoned the airline and booked himself on the next flight to the UK, laid his head back on the pillow and started fantasising about the woman who had inflicted his injuries. He chuckled to himself, he really needed to see a head doctor.

CHAPTER FORTY TWO

Pete called on April, suggesting that she should go away to see friends for a few days.

"What the hell has Charlie got into this time, and why isn't he talking to me?"

"Because he is flying back from New York right now."

"Should I really be worried?"

Pete took April's hand.

"Firstly, it's just a precaution and is probably something of nothing but if you are not here, neither of us will have to worry about you being drawn into it. So please just pack a week-ender and get away from here for a few days."

"And you will let me know what's happening?"

"Of course I will."

April said she would make some calls and see who would invite her to stay and let him know.

He then went to see Lily and Zoe. No surprise! Lily was out. Pete explained the situation to Zoe.

"Listen, Pete, we didn't mean for this to get dangerous."

"We know that, but that's the way things happen some time. Can you put the painting in the bank and can you give me a key for Lily's apartment?"

"Sure I will take the painting this morning while Lily is out. Why do you want the key?"

"You may have some unwanted visitors and we want to be ready for them."

Zoe looked worried.

"Pete, don't take any risks please. It's not worth it."

"It will be OK. We know what we are doing."

Zoe gave him a spare key.

"I will call you when I have made arrangements."

Pete got back to the office and made himself a cup of coffee and started the computer. The time read four thirty. He had to be at the airport in the morning for seven, so he needed to get an early night. He checked his emails, one jumped out at him.

'We note your interest in Henri Le Saux. Please phone at once.' The Surete.

Pete phoned the number and got an answer machine. He said he would be happy to speak to them and for them to call back after ten the following morning. He knew Charlie would have a plan and that trying to second guess him would be a waste of time, so he decided to call it a day and headed home.

Pete had collected Charlie, Julie and Ramon from the airport the following morning on time. Squeezing them and their luggage in the car was a triumph in itself. Pete had booked Julie and Ramon in to the George hotel, an old coaching inn in the centre of the city and a hundred yards from Charlie's office. They parked at the rear of the Hotel and Julie and Ramon checked in. Charlie and Pete went round to the office and opened up. As they got to the top of the stairs the phone started ringing.

"That will be the French police for you."

"What are you talking about?"

Pete told him about the email and said he had tried to phone them the day before.

"I'll call them later, but first I have a list of jobs for you to do."

Charlie told Pete what he needed.

"And what will you be doing while I'm working my tail off?"

"Giving our guests a tour of the city. We need to use Ramon to find out what the Chairman is up to but it doesn't mean we can trust him with our plans"

"You think this Chairman is a dangerous man then?"

"I think he is a desperate man and that makes him dangerous."

"And Henri Le Saux?"

"Oh, he really is dangerous especially after Thomas and Jordan ruffled his feathers."

"And he is on his way here?"

"The Chairman hasn't employed Ramon to do his dirty work for him so he will have instructed Le Saux to make his way here."

"So what's the plan Charlie?"

"Well I had seven hours on the plane to think about it, this is how I see it."

So Charlie told him.

CHAPTER FORTY THREE

Henri had arrived in London at lunchtime and rented a car. He programmed the navigation system and joined the M1 going north. He had called the Chairman when he picked up the car and would stay in the same hotel just south of the Lichfield. He hoped to be there before the afternoon was out.

Julie and Ramon had made their way to Charlie's office and they had had Ramon call the Chairman and tell him that he had arrived and asked for his instructions. The Chairman gave Ramon Charlie's office address and told him to make a note of the movements in and out. As Ramon was making the call from Charlie's office, this brought a smile to his face.

Charlie then told Julie and Ramon about the call from the French police.

"I really don't want the police involved for the next twenty four hours, so we need to placate them if we can."

Ramon nodded his head.

"I could speak to them if you would like?"

"That would be helpful. If you can explain that Pete and I are both ex police officers and that we will be consulting with our local police. "

Charlie dialled the number and passed the phone to Ramon. After much shrugging of shoulders and French expletives, he passed the phone back to Charlie.

"It is done but they expect this person Le Saux to be behind bars by tomorrow or you may cause a problem between our governments."

Charlie spent most the day showing Julie and Ramon the sights of Lichfield. He hadn't realised how much he knew about the city and how much he had taken for granted over the years. Ramon gave up asking why they were sight-seeing after the fourth time of asking. Charlie would only say that all would be revealed later on in the day. At five thirty they had had enough culture for one day. Charlie got Ramon to phone the Chairman and tell him the office appeared to have been locked up for the night and that he would re-commence his vigil at eight thirty the following morning. The Chairman agreed.

Pete had a busy day. This was punctuated by cursing Charlie under his breath. By six in the evening he was happy with his work and phoned Charlie.

"You really have no idea how to look after your data, do you?"

"I can find anything I want."

"You probably can but so can anyone else."

"So you sorted it out for me?"

"Yes and when this is sorted out, you will take instruction on how to protect your info."

Charlie put on a mock Chinese voice.

"Yes o wise one, the student follows the master."

"That's right. I'm the wise one and don't you forget it."

"I'll see you in half an hour at the restaurant."

"OK"

Charlie collected Julie and Ramon from the George Hotel and they walked to Charlie's favourite Indian restaurant. There were six or seven in the city centre but this one had a traditional Tandoor oven and had been at the same address for as long as Charlie could remember. Charlie was welcomed like an old friend by the owner. He asked if they could have a table by the window and as he sat down Pete walked through the door with a bag over his shoulder.

"Have you ordered yet, I'm famished."

Charlie noted Julie and Ramon's confusion on looking at the menu.

"The dish very popular here in the Midlands is the Balti, which comes in the dish it is cooked in."

Charlie pointed to the range of Balti options on the menu and they each picked one. Their drinks arrived and Charlie got up to speak to the owner who looked a little bemused but nodded his head in agreement.

Charlie sat down as Pete pulled a small portable TV out of his bag and switched it on. Julie and Ramon looked a bit affronted.

Charlie looked at Pete and winked at him.

"Pete, don't you think that it is a bit rude to bring your own TV to a restaurant when we have guests?"

"Normally I would agree but there is something I really must watch."

As he said this, he finished fine-tuning the picture and turned the screen to face the rest of the table.

The screen showed a black and white image of the interior of Charlie's office. Julie laughed. Ramon smiled and nodded his head.

"So now we wait?"

"Yes Ramon. Now we wait."

Le Saux arrived at the hotel and went to his room without telling the Chairman that he was there. He needed to take a shower and re-tape his injuries. He stripped and used the hot water to ease off the sticky tape. He had a purple and yellow bruise at the base of his rib cage, but that pain he could manage. It was the state of his feet that worried him. He couldn't put a foot down without wincing and the colour of them didn't look natural. He had suffered a lot of bruising in his life but never to this extent. He taped himself up and found a clean shirt in his bag. Forcing his feet back in his shoes, he stood up and looked at himself in the mirror. He would need some time to recover after this case was over. He looked ten years older than his age of thirty-one. He phoned reception and enquired as to the room number of the Chairman and went and knocked on his door.

"Good. You are here."

"What do you want me to do?"

The Chairman gave Le Saux Charlie's office address and told him he would accompany him. They left the hotel in Le Saux's rental car.

They pulled in to a car park one street away from the office.

"I will enter and call you if it is safe."

"Good I will await your call."

CHAPTER FORTY FOUR

They were served their food and ate while keeping one eye on the small screen. They took it in turns to tell tales of their respective lives in the police force. Charlie was warming to Ramon who appeared to have had a distinguished career in the Paris police. Julie took great pride in topping everyone's stories, which led Pete to start making some up.

Charlie tipped the wink to Ramon but Julie bought it hook, line and sinker. Finally Charlie couldn't take it any longer and started to laugh, then Ramon then Pete. Julie punched Pete on the shoulder and then laughed at herself.

Pete looked at the screen

"The game, as they say, is afoot."

Ramon shook his head

"I do not understand this 'afoot'."

Charlie nodded.

"Pete goes all 'Sherlock Holmes-ian' when he gets excited, take no notice!"

They watched as the shadowy figure started Charlie's computer, and rifled through the papers on his desk.

Charlie looked at Pete.

"I didn't have that much paper on my desk!"

"Professional licence made me do it. I wanted you to look like you were a busy little sleuth."

Charlie shook his head.

They all watched as Le Saux punched the keyboard. Pete smiled

"That's got him frustrated. Now look around. That's it. Well done."

Le Saux spotted the notation on the white board on the wall and took out his phone. He spoke for less than a minute.

"I have found something of interest, the door is on the latch, lock it behind you."

They waited. Suddenly Le Saux turned towards the stairs and then pointed at the board. A second figure came into view.

Charlie got up and paid the bill. Pete switched off the TV and stood up.

Julie and Ramon looked up from their seats.

Charlie turned to them and said

"Come on you two, as Thomas would say 'we have a party to go to'."

They filed out of the restaurant and walked towards Charlie's office.

Once outside Julie could contain herself no more.

"OK. Charlie what's the plan?"

So Charlie told them.

Charlie and Pete strolled up the street talking in an absent-minded way and got to the office door Charlie unlocked the door and they climbed the stairs still chattering away about nothing. As Charlie's head came out of the stair well, Le Saux threw a punch but Charlie had expected it and ducked to the side. He grabbed Le Saux's wrist and twisted it, forcing his arm to straighten and pushing Le Saux back into the room. Stumbling into the Chairman, they both ended in a heap on the floor. Le Saux winced with pain and dragged himself to his feet. Pete got to the top of the stairs to see Le Saux pull a kitchen knife out of his pocket. Pete reached into his bag.

"Handy with a knife, are you?"

Le Saux just smiled. Pete smiled back and produced a revolver from his bag. The Chairman cursed in French and crawled away to the corner of the room. Le Saux's smile dropped for a moment then came back.

"This is England, mon ami. You will not use it, if it works at all."

Pete raised the gun towards Le Saux.

"Last chance, put the knife down now."

Le Saux smiled

"No"

Pete squeezed the trigger. Click. Pete turned to Charlie.

"You did say it wouldn't work."

Charlie shrugged.

"It was worth a try."

He turned to Le Saux.

"Well Henri, how long have you been working for the Chairman?"

Le Saux' glanced at the figure cowering in the corner and back at Charlie.

"I do not know this man."

"He is the Chairman."

Another French expletive came from the corner.

"You fool, get us out of here."

"Well get up then."

The Chairman got up and stood behind Le Saux, getting his composure back.

Charlie stood his ground.

"Are you intending to put us in a coma like the old man in New York?"

The Chairman looked at Le Saux.

"What are they talking about?"

"It was an accident, a little collateral damage that is all."

"The New York police view it in a different light."

The Chairman went ashen.

"I only wanted you to put pressure on people, not kill them."

"You instructed me to get the copies by any means possible."

Charlie gave a little chuckle.

"Well now we know your relationship, what about Ramon Ducat?"

The Chairman grimaced

"He is nothing but a bumbling fool, a waste of time."

Charlie smiled

Le Saux took a step toward Charlie, pointing the knife at his throat.

"Out of our way"

Charlie shrugged and stepped to the side

Pete got out his phone and pressed a speed dial number.

"When you are ready, no need for sirens, yes that's right."

Le Saux looked aghast.

"Another bluff"

Pete smiled

"You will be arrested for breaking and entering and then the Americans and the French will fight over who will extradite you."

Charlie gestured towards the Chairman.

"You will be arrested as his accomplice and for ordering the assault in America. So that will be your business life over."

Le Saux looked at the Chairman

"We must leave now."

The Chairman nodded. Le Saux pointed at the stairs and the Chairman went down them first. Le Saux backed down the stairs pointing the knife at Charlie who followed. The Chairman opened the door and stepped outside without looking. Ramon grabbed his arm and swung him round face first into front of the charity shop window. The window cracked but didn't break which was more than could be said for the Chairman's nose. Blood ran down the window and on to the sill.

"A bumbling fool, am I?"

As this happened Le Saux stepped through the doorway. Realising that the Chairman wasn't going anywhere, he decided to make a run for it. He turned and took two strides down the street. A foot came out of a doorway and tripped him up. He winced and rolled on to his back. Julie stood over him.

"OK. You have had your fun but it's over."

Julie didn't know he had a knife. He sat up in a resigned manner then stabbed her in the thigh. Charlie came out of the door in time to see Julie fall to the floor and Le Saux get to his feet and start running. Charlie bent down over Julie she gasped

"I am OK. Go get the bastard."

Le Saux didn't know where he was going except that it was away from his car. He needed to double back on himself. He ran into the market square and could hear running feet behind him. The city was quiet at this time of the evening, before the night-time revellers arrived. He told himself just keep turning left and you will come back to the car park. He turned into Dam Street and continued to run. The running feet behind were getting closer. If he got to his car then he needed to get away without the chance of the number being taken. He decided to confront the running feet before he got to the car park. The first left turn he came to ran along the side of a pool in the shadow of the cathedral. There were trees and less street lighting, he would wait here for his prey. The running feet approached.

Charlie knew he was gaining on Le Saux, but where did he think he was going? He turned on to the path that ran by the side of Minster pool. He couldn't see him or hear him running. At the same time as Charlie's internal warning light flickered in his brain, he caught a movement to his left. Le Saux darted from behind a tree, knife raised. Charlie tried to sidestep the blow but felt the blade of the knife slice through his jacket and enter his forearm. Le Saux grabbed Charlie round the throat from behind and pulled him towards him with his free hand and raise the knife with the intention of plunging it into Charlie's throat. In retrospect Charlie marvelled at the amount of time he had to think about what to do, considering it was all over in less than thirty seconds. Remembering his police training he became a dead weight, leaning back on his assailant forcing him to take a step back to gain his balance. What happened next surprised Charlie the most. As Charlie took another step back to keep the momentum going he trod on Le Saux's instep. The reaction was a deafening scream in Charlie's ear. The knife clattered onto the path. Le Saux hopped, off balance, to the water's edge, where he crashed into the thigh-high railing and over into the pool. The sleeping ducks and guinea fowl adding to the commotion.

Charlie watched Le Saux flounder trying to find his footing, slipping on the side of the pool and falling back into the water again.

Charlie had his hands on his knees, trying to get his breath back when two of his former colleagues came running along the path.

"Not as fit as you used to be, Charlie?"

"Sod off."

"That's no way to speak to the Police, now is it?"

"OK. Arrest him for breaking and entering, actual bodily harm and attempted murder."

Charlie pointed to the knife on the path.

"That's the weapon involved and he was some sort of Special Forces, so be careful."

"I don't know Charlie, sounds like a lot of paperwork to us!"

Le Saux had dragged himself out of the pool and had one leg over the railing. One of the policemen held out a hand to help him. As soon as Le Saux held his hand out, he cuffed his wrist and tried to turn it behind his back. Le Saux pulled the officer towards him and deposited him in the Pool. Charlie stamped on Le Saux's foot again causing him to fall against the railing, so Charlie took the opportunity to cuff him to the ironwork.

Charlie looked at the Officer standing waist-deep in water.

"I told you to be careful."

"Sod off" was the reply.

Charlie started to walk back to his office.

"You are lucky I don't report you to the Chief Constable talking to a respected member of the community like that!"

He turned the corner before he could hear the response.

Charlie approached his office to see two police cars and an ambulance outside. Julie was inside on a stretcher. The Chairman sat on the back step holding a wad of cotton wool to his nose. Charlie ignored the Chairman and climbed past him into the ambulance.

"How are you doing?"

"OK. It's deep but not life threatening."

"Looks like you may be here for a few days then."

"Ten years as a cop and PI in New York and nothing like this has happened to me and I come to England and I get stabbed. Go figure. They reckon they will want me to stay in hospital overnight and then keep my weight off it for a couple of weeks."

After the wound on Charlie's arm had been dressed, the driver said they had to leave so he got out and helped the Chairman stand up. Charlie could see that he was still in shock after being manhandled by Ramon.

"Have they asked you any questions?"

"Not yet."

"Good because this is what I want you to tell them. If you do as I say you will not go to prison. But at any time if you do not do as I say, I will ruin your name."

"How can you do that?"

"I have everything that happened in my office on film."

The Chairman looked defeated.

"Come on we had better go up to the office and see how Pete's getting on with our detective inspector."

"Merde!"

"Why so down? You never know this could be the start of a beautiful friendship!"

EPILOGUE

Charlie, Pete and Julie walked past the glass pyramid, the rain running in sheets down its sides. Julie was walking again even though her leg was stiff with lack of use. Pete was chattering away to Julie about Paris and Charlie reflected on the four weeks since the arrest of Henri LeSaux.

With the good news that James Adams had recovered and apart from having to have his jaw wired up for another two weeks he would be fine. As a result of his recovery, the American authorities had not pushed for Le Saux's extradition as he had a string of charges awaiting him in France.

Charlie had sat down with the Chairman and explained how things should be presented to the world at large. This would let the Chairman of the hook, which rankled with Julie, as she hated the injustice of the situation. Charlie explained that his way would benefit all the owners of the paintings.

The idea was simple. The Trust would have completed its task once all the copies had been found and tested. This had now taken place and the original established. The owner would be revealed in the Louvre today. Charlie proposed that the four copies and the story of their history would be taken on a world-wide tour. This would be a joint venture between the members of the Trust, the Louvre and the owners of the paintings, generating income for all of the owners. The Chairman liked the idea and got agreement and support from the other members of the Trust and the Louvre for the venture.

Charlie also wanted a further two people to benefit from the enterprise, James Adams and Lady Sinclair. The Chairman started to object but Charlie just smiled at him and the Chairman nodded in agreement. The Louvre looked upon the proposal as a win-win opportunity, finally putting to bed the doubt over their

Mona Lisa and mounting an exhibition that would generate considerable income. The owners of the paintings and those to benefit from the proceeds had arrived in Paris the day before and handed over their paintings to be prepared for the opening of the exhibition.

They entered via the main entrance and a throng of people turned to greet them. First to step forward was Richard Carboni with Thomas standing at his shoulder.

"Charlie Edwards, I need to know if your intentions towards my daughter Jordan are honourable?"

Charlie went as white as a sheet. Then Thomas began to giggle.

"You got him with that one boss."

Carboni's face broke out in a big smile as he grabbed Charlie and gave him a big hug.

"It was Thomas's idea. You should have seen your face!"

Charlie introduced Julie and Pete.

Thomas giggled.

"So this is the brains of the outfit?"

Pete was warming to Thomas, pointed at Julie.

"No she's the brains, I'm the beauty."

Thomas stepped aside and introduced James Adams.

"He came across with us."

They all shook hands and Charlie spoke to him.

"I'm very sorry you were put through this ordeal. I do hope you will be ok?"

Through a clenched jaw he said he was on the mend and expected to make a full recovery. Thomas patted him on the back.

"Yeah, he has promised to give me piano lessons when he recovers."

Thomas flexed the digits on his meat plate sized hands. James smiled and looked at the heavens, shaking his head. Teresa Clarke and Al walked up and Charlie did the introductions leaving Pete till last.

"Oh so this is Pete! Did you enjoy the photo I sent you?"

Pete coloured up and stammered a response in the affirmative.

"Good, there's plenty more where they came from. I will send you some more."

Pete stammered his thanks and they were all asked to walk through into a reception room, where canapés and champagne were served. They waved to Zoe and Lily as they moved forward, Zoe on Richard Carboni's arm, Lily parting the crowd with her scooter. Zoe would never be one to miss an opportunity.

As they were offered a drink, Lady Sinclair and Agnes approached.

"Well young man you appear to have done very well for us all and I would like to thank you."
Charlie went to reply but was grabbed and kissed on the cheek leaving a bright red lipstick mark. Lady Sinclair giggled and Agnes started to rebuke her.

"I told you not to attack the mini bar in the hotel before we came. Now you have embarrassed the young man."

"You are just jealous, as you are with all my conquests."

Charlie interrupted them.

"Agnes, don't I get a kiss from you?"

Charlie bent down and she kissed him on the other cheek, so that now he had a matching pair of lips on both cheeks. Lady Sinclair and Agnes started argue about who Charlie preferred while wandering off in search of a refill. Charlie looked at the expression on Pete and Julie's face. He gave a little shrug.

"You have either got it or you haven't."

Julie laughed.

"It's what you have got that we are trying to figure out."

As Charlie turned back to the room Hans and Klaus stood in front of him and both gave a little bow. Hans spoke.

"It is good to see you again Charlie." They exchanged hearty handshakes and Charlie again made the introductions. Klaus spoke.

"So today we will see who is the winner."

"I hope everybody will be the winner."

"Yes but someone will win more than the others. Ja?"

Charlie reflected that all four owners had agreed on a sum with the Louvre, should one of their paintings turn out to be the original.

Hans looked slightly embarrassed at his companion.

"Klaus has a very competitive nature which has gotten him in trouble in his youth."

Klaus coloured up and offered to get everybody another glass of bubbly.

Hans stepped closer to Charlie.

"I have decided to take your advice and take a holiday once the wine harvest is completed. My uncle lived in Mallorca after the war and kept a diary which is all I have of his, so I thought I would take it back to Mallorca and see the island through his eyes."

Charlie couldn't at first remember giving the advice but was happy he would break the cycle of his life and start living again.

"I am really pleased for you."

"Thank you."

At that point Klaus returned with five glasses and the large doors at the end of the room opened. A man in a tailcoat announced that they should all proceed through to the next room. Everybody filed through, each of them gasping at the sight in front of them. Five Mona Lisas.

Ramon Ducat, appointed as security consultant for the paintings, stood on a small podium next to the pictures and behind him stood members of the Trust and officials of the Louvre. He spoke in French and then in English.

"Ladies and Gentlemen, you can see the Louvre Mona Lisa and your four paintings are arranged around it. You were given a number for your painting, one to four. I'll ask the curator to now place the real Mona Lisa in the centre frame."

They all watched as the central Mona Lisa was removed and replaced by...

There was a swoon and the sound of someone hitting the floor. Everybody turned to see who it was.

Thomas gave a little giggle.

The next day, the sun shone down on Charlie, Julie and Pete as they strolled across the Market Square in Lichfield, on their way to induct Julie into the ways of their favourite watering hole. Pete gave Charlie a little nudge.

"See that guy over there?"

"Yes"

"He is about to discover something about the human body that has defeated man for hundreds of years!"

"What are you talking about? All he is doing is eating an ice cream, admittedly he isn't very good at it, and it's running all over his hand."

"Just watch and be amazed!"

They watched as the man got into a mess, ice cream running down his wrist, down his fore arm, the first trickle of the melted confection reaching his elbow.

"Here we go, watch this."

The first sticky drop dripped of the point of his elbow. Prompting the man to transfer the ice cream to his other hand. He then proceeded to lick the ice cream of his wrist, forearm and elbow. But he can't reach the point of his elbow with his tongue. He tried again nearly dislocating his shoulder in the process. That was when he realised that people were watching him and scurried off.

"You see, man cannot lick his own elbow."

"Now we know the same piece of useless information you do!"

"Come on, you can buy me a pint for enriching your lives."

Pete strode off in front of Charlie and Julie and without looking back said, "do you know how silly you both look right now?"

Charlie and Julie put their elbows by their sides and looked sheepishly at each other. Then Julie laughed.

"I'll lick yours if you lick mine."

"Let discuss that this evening."

Pete had already ordered for them as they got to the bar, he gathered up the three drinks and left Charlie to pay.

They sat in a booth and each took a draft from their pint. Pete turned to Julie.

"So you are heading home tomorrow?"

"Yes. The publicity of the case has created interest and Alex is excited about some of the potential clients."

"Well if we can be of help, give us a call."

"Charlie and I are going to talk about that tonight over dinner."

Pete said rather grandly "yes sorry I cannot join you but I have a prior engagement."

Charlie looking down at his pint.

"Yes. Give Mother my love."

Silence.

Pete thought about denial but knew it was futile.

"How long have you known?"

"For sure about thirty seconds ago."

"You sod!"

"You didn't ask me where Mother lived, when I asked you to look after the garden."

"There are lots of ways to find out where she lived?"

"Yes but none as natural as asking me!"

Charlie looked up from his pint.

"Pete, are your intentions honourable?"

"You are a bigger wind-up merchant than me!"

Charlie laughed. "And don't you ever forget it."

They all laughed

Pete took another pull on his pint.

"Have you spoken to Lily and Zoe?"

"Yes they are sorting out the inheritance with the lawyers today. Zoe and Richard Carboni have taken a personal interest in the operation of the paintings tour and Zoe will manage the events."

"What about Lily?"

"Oh she will go with Zoe on the tour. Travelling the world on her little scooter."

"That Zoe doesn't let the dust settle, does she?"

"She likes to be in control, that's for sure."

Pete looked at his empty glass and looked at Charlie.

"Ok I'll get another round."

While Charlie was at the bar Pete had a phone call. He put his phone away just as Charlie returned.

"What was that about?"

"Someone I haven't heard from in thirty odd years. Old school friend, never really got on but wants me to help him decipher some script he found on a piece of metal he found in a field. He's a metal-detectorist. Said it looks like ancient Greek."

"Sound intriguing."

They sat in silence enjoying their pints and wondering about the opportunities lying in front of them.

Pete, with his piece of metal.

Julie, with her new business opportunities.

Charlie with Julie. He knew the answer machine in the office was full. It would still be full tomorrow. Priorities. Priorities.

I hope no-one has done themselves a mischief, trying to lick their elbows! Have you figured out who inherited the original painting? All the clues are there.

Although the historical portion of the book is based on fact, this is a book of fiction and events have been embellished to enhance the plot. All the characters in the rest of the book are a work of my imagination.

If you have enjoyed the book then please do let me know at www.enjoyagoodread.com , where you can read about the further adventures of Charlie and Peter.

Carl R Stokes